"There is wondrous magic to be found in this world," Bain said softly, "if you will but believe...."

He crushed his mouth over Caitlin's, and her arms wound around his neck as though they belonged there. A faint voice asked what she thought she was doing, giving herself to this stranger, this mysterious midnight rider.

And why didn't she care?

All she cared for was the taste of his mouth, the feel of his flesh against her fingers, the beat of his heart as it sang with hers. When his hand slipped down to the opening of her robe, his fingers left a trail of fire.

Fairy fire.

But then he pushed her away. "That should not have happened," he muttered. "We cannot be together."

"Why not?" she cried, shaken.

When he spoke again, his expression was bleak. "I, lady, am lost in a darkness from which there is no escape...."

Dear Reader,

Welcome back to the dark side of love. As we wind up our first year of publication, we're proud to bring you one author whose first Shadows novel appeared in our very first month and equally proud to offer you the first of what we hope will be many spooky tales by an author team new to the line.

Carla Cassidy's *Silent Screams* is just as scary as you'd expect it to be, coming from the author of *Swamp Secrets* and *Heart of the Beast*. It's a story of ghostly possession, and it takes place in an old mansion whose walls—if only they could talk—could tell tales of murder and betrayal and love everlasting. You, too, may scream—and not silently!—as you turn the pages.

Next up is *The Prince of Air and Darkness*, by two authors who write as Jeanne Rose. This is a wonderful blend of reality and myth and irresistible romance, a heady concoction that will stay with you long after you've finished the last chapter and set the book aside. And isn't that what haunting's really all about?

In months to come, as we start on Year Two, we'll be back with more of the wonderful mix of passion and peril that has come to mean reading pleasure to book lovers everywhere, the wonderful mix that is Silhouette Shadows. Until then—enjoy!

Leslie Wainger
Senior Editor and Editorial Coordinator

Please address questions and book requests to:
Reader Service
U.S.: P.O. Box 1325, Buffalo, NY 14269
Canadian: P.O. Box 1050, Niagara Falls, Ont. L2E 7G7

JEANNE ROSE

THE PRINCE OF AIR AND DARKNESS

SILHOUETTE® Shadows™

Published by Silhouette Books
America's Publisher of Contemporary Romance

SILHOUETTE BOOKS

ISBN 0-373-27026-7

THE PRINCE OF AIR AND DARKNESS

Books by Jeanne Rose

Silhouette Shadows
The Prince of Air and Darkness #26

Silhouette Romance
Believing in Angels #913

JEANNE ROSE

is the newest pseudonym of Patricia Pinianski and Linda Sweeney. The Chicagoans have been a team since 1982, when they met in a writing class. Now Linda teaches writing at two suburban community colleges and works for *Writer's Digest,* while Patricia makes writing her full-time focus. Patricia and Linda are happy they can combine their fascination with the mysterious and magical with their belief in the triumph of love. Patricia and Linda are also known as Lynn Patrick, and Patricia writes as Patricia Rosemoor.

Thanks to Leslie Wainger and Risa Kessler
and readers who want mystery and magic
with their romance

PROLOGUE

The small parcel looked quite ordinary, he thought with satisfaction as he carried his newest purchase into the study. No one would guess the power and the means to riches that lay beneath the ordinary brown-paper wrapping...not even the used-book seller. The merchant had been interested only in the extravagant price he'd been able to garner.

Though eager to examine his treasure, he first carefully bolted the door and pulled the heavy curtains across the room's single large window. He required utmost privacy for this intellectual sojourn into the past. The compendium he'd been seeking for a decade held the key to his future.

Sitting at the polished oak desk, he slit open the wrapping with a pair of antique silver scissors. His hands trembled slightly as he removed the ancient leather-bound volume embossed with intricately twined gold leaf. The pages inside were yellowed with age, and the dust made his hands itch and his nose quiver. He paid the small inconveniences no mind.

Rather, he pored over the first paragraph:

> The Ogham Alphabet was especially favoured by the Celts of pre-Christian times, when it was used for magical and divinatory purposes...

Nothing new here. Impatient, he thumbed further into the book, until he found the alphabet itself. Gazing over the series of strokes arranged on either side of a dividing line brought a smile of gratification to his lips. Runes. Never before had he seen such a complete, beautifully defined set. Eagerly he continued on.

The last section of the book contained the magical quatrains.

Once more he was ready to carry on the quest. Laying the book down carefully, he took a key from the desk drawer and rose to unlock the carved wooden cabinet sitting against the north wall. He ran his fingers over the wands of hazel wood and blackthorn— basic tools for the adept—but passed over them to choose the silk-shrouded casket and the sheathed dagger, both of which he carried back to the desk.

A ragged map lay at the bottom of the casket. Finally it would serve its true purpose. He opened the book again, searching for the legendary quatrain. Upon finding it, he shouted in triumph and read aloud in Gaelic:

His sword shall not pierce;
His wrath shall not burn;
His word shall not halt;
His power shall not carry in either world.
By the power of this spell, such is the lot of The Prince of Air and Darkness.

At last he had the edge. At last he would prevail. Nothing would stop him now.

CHAPTER ONE

Midnight. Fog. Darkness palpable enough to touch.

Caitlin Montgomery shivered. Deciding she'd had enough of Scottish country ambience, she turned up the rental car's heater to drive away the damp night chill. The small vehicle inched along the steep, winding road, its headlights barely cutting through the drifting mist. Knowing that sheer drops might lurk on either side, that the car could too easily drop off the road and into a narrow saltwater loch, made Caitlin nervous. In this rugged area of western Scotland called Strathclyde, the land was deeply penetrated and chopped by the sea.

What she wouldn't give to be home right now, cruising a nice multilane California freeway with plenty of highway lights and bright neon signs advertising restaurants and bars. She'd never experienced such a spooky sense of total aloneness, not even when driving through a seedy part of Santa Barbara by herself.

Her shoulders were beginning to ache from hunching over the wheel. And, though the night was cold, she was so tired that she had to keep a window cracked to remain alert.

If only she hadn't stayed so long in Inveraray. She should have started back for the village of Droon, and her bed-and-breakfast, hours earlier, before the fog had settled over the coast. But she'd had such a fascinating time exploring an old graveyard and sketching the stones, then visiting with some locals at a pub afterward, that she'd forgotten the time.

She shoved the car into second as it groaned up an incline, then slowed the vehicle when the mist cleared at the top. The fog had been hiding a dim, faraway moon whose glow revealed the craggy black shapes of mountains in the distance, strips of open water, and, closer, the dark outline of low stone walls enclosing fields of heather and gorse.

Caitlin peered closely, trying to catch any stray pinprick of light. She'd spotted a couple of thatch-roofed crofts when she'd driven in the opposite direction that morning. Nothing visible now. Too bad. The presence of other people in the vicinity would have made her feel better.

Safer.

The car nosed back into the fog and rolled downhill. When the engine coughed, Caitlin immediately switched into neutral and gunned the accelerator. All she needed was to be stranded out here in the middle of nowhere late into the night!

At least it was only the steep roads that were dangerous, she assured herself. No muggers or drug addicts—or crazy would-be suitors—lurking about. Her feeling of unease might be due to the newness of the foreign setting. Since she'd arrived in the British Isles mere days before, she was used to neither the steering wheel being on the right side nor the one-lane rural roads.

Caitlin looked for landmarks through each break in the fog. Nearby lay a circle of cairns, ancient Celtic burial mounds. Beyond, perched on a rocky promontory above the sea, were the massive ruins of a legendary castle called Black Broch. The mist swirled again, and she sighed with relief when she caught a glimpse of the Halt sign at the corner of the intersection. At last! On the other side of the road stood a bigger sign pointing toward Droon. Soon she'd be safe and warm in her bed.

But as the car crawled to a stop, the engine coughed again, then sputtered into silence.

"What?" Annoyed and disbelieving, Caitlin turned the key in the ignition. Nothing. "I can't be out of gas!" Not when the gauge showed the tank was half-full. And there couldn't be anything wrong with the battery, or the headlights wouldn't be blazing. "You can't be stalled!" She tried the ignition again.

Click, click. Click, click.

Definitely stalled. "Damn!" She hit the steering wheel with the flat of her hand.

What a mess! Nearly a mile to Droon, and no one else driving by. What to do? Caitlin stubbornly tried to start the car one last time, clenching her jaw when it wouldn't cooperate. Putting it in neutral, she got out and pushed the vehicle onto the gravel shoulder. What a night! She wouldn't get to bed until the wee hours of the morning.

Cursing, she grabbed her sketchbook and stuck it in her purse, then slung the bag over her shoulder and tightened her lightweight blue trench coat, wishing she'd worn a thicker sweater underneath, one of good Scots wool. The creak of the Crossroads sign in the breeze made her shiver. She was reluctant to turn the car's headlights off and enshroud herself completely in darkness. She didn't even have a flashlight.

Suddenly, through the fog, came the soft *clop, clop* of approaching hoofbeats.

A pony cart, perhaps? That throwback to an earlier time was not an uncommon sight in rural Scotland. Her spirits rising, Caitlin called, "Hello? Is somebody there?"

No answer. But a form took shape beyond the beam of the headlights—the tall, shadowy silhouette of a man on horseback. She backed up when the horse and rider stepped right out of the fog. Steam rose from the great shimmering beast's nostrils, and his eyes glowed red as he pranced directly toward her.

"Ahh!" She stumbled farther back, flattening herself against the car.

The black horse snorted and tossed his head when his heavily cloaked rider sharply drew in the reins. She could almost imagine she was gazing at a vision. Were the animal's eyes really red? And what kind of face was the rider's cloak hiding? A skull, perhaps?

Goose bumps rose along her skin. Her heart pounded. She suddenly remembered the superstitious housekeeper's warning that very morning at breakfast: "Nae be gettin' caught at a crossroads in the midst o' the night, or the divil hisself'll take ye."

What a comforting thought. Then again, if the apparition was indeed the devil, he could give her a lift somewhere. Despite her attempt at humor, she flinched when the rider started to pull back his high collar. But the face revealed by the lights of her small car was that of a man—a very handsome man, with dark, wind-blown hair and chiseled features.

He frowned down at her. "Are you ill, lady?" His voice was deep, his accent more cultured British than Scottish brogue.

Caitlin shook her head and let her breathing slow as she realized she'd let her imagination get away from her. How ridiculous. The rider was a human being, not the devil, and his horse's eyes had only glowed red because they reflected the headlights.

She finally managed to point at the vehicle. "My car's ill, not me."

His brooding frown didn't waver. "And what might you be doing out here this night?"

"Isn't it obvious? The engine died. I'm stranded."

He glanced about. "You are alone?"

Suddenly uncomfortable, she quickly said, "I'm on my way to the MacDonald Bed and Breakfast, near Droon. The owners are expecting me." A small white lie, but one that made her feel better. "Do you know anybody around here who has a phone? I'll get someone to come and pick me up."

"I have no knowledge of my neighbors."

"Well, what about *you?*" she asked reluctantly. "Can I use your telephone?"

Though she wasn't certain she wanted to enter this man's abode. He might be fully human, and devastatingly handsome, but something about him frightened her... an air of danger. Surely this man had sensed her fear when he appeared out of the mist, and yet he'd done nothing to assuage her uneasiness.

He told her, "I own very few modern conveniences."

"And I suppose that means you're no good at fixing cars."

His horse stirred restlessly, and he shifted the reins. His intense blue eyes, startling in contrast with his dark hair, flicked over her. "Are you truly alone, lady?"

Wishing she could say she had an army of friends nearby, Caitlin inched her hand toward the door handle. Her instincts told her to be on guard. "Why?"

"I have had problems with trespassers of late."

So that explained his unsmiling watchfulness. She sagged with relief and dropped her hand. "Don't worry, I'm no trespasser. I merely want to get to my lodgings. Looks like I'm going to have to walk." She glanced at the car's dimming headlights. "And if I don't watch out, I'll have a dead battery, as well as whatever else is wrong with this bucket of bolts."

As she opened the door to turn the lights off, she felt edgy. Now she would be alone in the dark with the brooding stranger. At least the mist was starting to lift. The black shape of the horse and rider loomed in pale moonlight, then edged closer with a creak of leather and a jingle of bit.

"I will take you to your lodgings," he stated, reaching down for her.

She stepped back, her heart pounding again inordinately hard. But then, she had reason to be wary of aggressive strangers. "Uh, I don't ride."

"But I do. You need only sit in front of me." He already had an iron grip on her wrist and was pulling her toward him. "Put your foot in the stirrup and jump up."

An order, not a suggestion. She tried to jerk away. "No, really..."

But he didn't let go. "You are very strong-willed."

"I told you, I don't ride."

"You will reach your lodgings much faster on horseback than on foot." He laughed softly, and his slight accent thickened for a moment as he said, "I mean you no harm, lass."

"I'm not so sure about that."

"My offer was meant to be chivalrous, not threatening." He slid his booted foot out of the stirrup. "Allow me to take you to your lodgings."

Without waiting, he lifted her and seated her before him, sideways, so her legs dangled against one of his. The hard muscles of his chest pressed into her softer flesh, and his breath was warm against her nape as he reined the animal and turned it toward Droon. Caitlin's nerves fluttered, and she squirmed, trying to get comfortable, fully aware of the man's warm, hard thighs pressing into her bottom.

"Hold on to me," he commanded.

She had no choice, if she wanted to maintain her balance. She slid an arm beneath his cloak and about his waist. She judged him to be fairly tall, over six feet, and he was lean and hard with muscle.

The horse tossed its head and lengthened its stride until they were galloping. Holding on to the rider with one arm and a handful of mane with her free hand, Caitlin felt as if she were flying through some kind of wild, romantic dream. The road to Droon skirted the sea—on one side, the moon-silvered hills and glens slid past like magic, while on the other, waves sang at the foot of sheer, rocky cliffs.

Earth and water.

The wind fluttered the rider's cloak behind and about them. High above, thousands of stars flamed in stunning glory.

Fire and air.

But the ride was far from some dream. Aware of the flexing muscles of the galloping animal beneath her, hearing the rhythm of the pounding hooves, Caitlin was also all too conscious of the physical presence of the man in whose arms she rested.

Flesh and blood.

The ride would be over too soon, she thought.

Though she hadn't told him where the MacDonald place was located, the stranger headed his horse in the correct direction. How odd, after his insisting he had no knowledge of his neighbors. Perhaps he meant personal knowledge, she told herself. That didn't mean he wouldn't know who lived where. He slowed his mount as he turned it onto the gravel road that led up to the manor.

The magic had to end. Indicating her guest cottage, beyond the larger building, she broke the spell. "Over there."

He guided the horse to her doorstep and reined it to a halt.

"I trust I have delivered you whole and unharmed."

"Yes. Thank you."

He took hold of her chin and turned her face toward him. When he spoke, his accent came to the fore again. "You had no need to fear my mount...or me, lass."

Reaction from his touch shuddered through her as she said, "The name's Caitlin Montgomery."

His eyes were shadowed, yet she imagined they blazed with more than a passing interest as he said, "A lovely name for a lovely and spirited woman."

His voice was low and throbbing, and it affected her far more than she might have liked. Whispers of heat fluttered through her. He was a stranger, for heaven's sake, and she didn't know anything about him. Remembering the last time she'd been so attracted to a man—another mysterious man who'd proven to be dangerous —she tried to wiggle free, but he held her fast about the waist.

"Good night," she said pointedly. "I'm sure we'll run into each other, since you live around here."

He acted as if he had no intention of letting her go. His finger gently traced her lower lip, making her insides tighten. "If you truly want to see me again, you shall."

"Is there some reason I *shouldn't* want to see you?" Caitlin struggled with herself—her reaction was definitely inappropriate—and searched for the determination she was famous for. "Have you got a bad reputation or something?"

"Some would say so."

She firmly pushed at his restraining arm until she could slide down from the saddle ... only to have him stop her as she dropped. He had hold of her waist again, though this time she was turned and pulled against him, her feet dangling. She was amazed at his strength. And at her inability to object in an effective manner.

"Here's to whether we meet again or no."

Without giving her time to think, he covered her mouth with a searching kiss. It was sheer instinct that opened Caitlin's lips, that allowed her to share his breath. As their tongues touched, her back arched and she wound her arms about his neck. Heat spread from her middle, making her blood sing. But the kiss was over as swiftly as it had begun. With another soft laugh, the mounted stranger let her slide to the ground. Feeling oddly dizzy, she nearly stumbled as he rode away.

A minute or two later, she had located her keys and let herself into the cottage. Fearing the lights would nearly blind her, she made her way through the shadows and collapsed on the bed. As she lay there, tired but now strangely wakeful, she would have sworn she could still hear hoofbeats.

She touched her lips in remembrance of the kiss and wondered what had possessed her to let a man whose name she didn't even know get so close.

When Caitlin opened her eyes again, bright sunlight was streaming through the cottage windows. She groaned and turned over, stiff and sore from sleeping on top of the bedspread fully dressed. She couldn't remember falling asleep. She also wasn't sure if she'd actually hitched a moonlight ride with a nameless man on horseback the night before, or if she'd dreamed the whole episode.

Surely something uncommon had happened, or she wouldn't be lying there in her trench coat.

She rose slowly, groaning again, and went to the window to see if her car was parked outside. The drive was empty.

So she *had* hitched a ride.

And she certainly had been kissed.

The clock showed 9:20—she was still in time for breakfast. Hungry, Caitlin washed up, ran a brush through her hair and pulled on fresh clothing, then headed for the main house. Outside, she examined the damp earth and gravel for hoofprints, and was puzzled when she couldn't seem to find any.

Entering the manor's spacious entryway, she made her way down the hall. Several guests sat in the dining room beyond. The older American couple, the silver-haired Professor Abernathy and his petite wife, were carrying on a lively conversation with the MacDonalds and Julian Taylor, the London antique dealer, all of whom Caitlin had met when she first arrived.

"Don't think I'm not careful of the people I take in," Mary MacDonald said firmly. "I accept only those who are referred by the agency in Glasgow. I don't want the riffraff. Why, Sally Campbell had an antique chest taken from her own home in Droon! And right beneath her very nose, too."

Mrs. Abernathy clucked. "How terrible."

Mary addressed Julian. "And have you ever been approached with such goods in your store?"

"Stolen articles?" Julian paused. "It's hard to say for certain, but I hope not. I'd wager the thief who took that chest wanted it for himself."

"Nevertheless, you have to be careful," Professor Abernathy put in, between puffs on his pipe. "There are those who would steal the Loch Ness monster if they could get hold of it."

Alistair MacDonald didn't react to the other man's humor. His rugged, mustached face wore a disapproving expression. "I met a man in Greece once who was carrying around a huge chunk of marble column in his luggage."

Julian shook his sleek head. Then he spotted Caitlin coming toward the group and broke into a smile. "Well, good morning, Miss Montgomery."

"Caitlin," she said. "Good morning, everyone."

"Yes. 'Tis a glorious day we'll be having, after the damp and fog of last eve," Mary said.

Julian rose and pulled out a chair for her. "You're looking lovely, as usual."

"Thank you."

Yesterday, Julian had gone out of his way to praise her rich auburn "Highland" hair after she admitted having a Scottish grandfather. Sitting, she spotted the platter of scones in the middle of the table. Her mouth watered.

"Is there any coffee left?" she asked Bridget, the plump cook and housekeeper.

"Aye, an' some eggs, and a wee bit o' bacon, too, if ye will."

"I know I should have been a bit more prompt."

Mary waved an elegant ringed hand. "Don't be worrying yourself. A vacation's for relaxing. No strict schedules."

Caitlin smiled. "That's very gracious of you."

"Living graciously is what we like to do best," said Alistair.

Caitlin was certain that was the truth, just as she was certain the MacDonalds didn't really need the extra income from the bed-and-breakfast. A successful middle-aged businessman who'd retired early from his export-import business, Alistair had told her he now divided his time between his hobby of studying Scotland's history and legends and joining his talkative wife in playing host to international visitors.

As soon as Bridget brought her a cup of coffee, Caitlin helped herself to a scone and slathered it with butter.

"Late night?" Julian asked.

"I left Inveraray later than I expected, and got caught in the fog."

"Find something fascinating in the town?"

She nodded. "Old tombstones with Celtic designs. I did several sketches."

"And you'll turn them into exquisite jewelry, I imagine," said Mary, smoothing a stray brown hair into her chignon. She turned to Mrs. Abernathy. "Caitlin is a famous artist."

Caitlin laughed. "I only wish I were famous." She'd been lucky enough to sell a line of jewelry to a department-store chain the year before, but her career as a designer had barely taken off. "I'm merely doing well."

Well enough to please herself, at any rate. After years of pursuing her interest as a hobby and selling at craft fairs, she was finally able to concentrate on designing full-time. As well as a badly needed change of pace, this research trip was a chance to get ideas for a new line that would allow her to explore Scotland's past. She had always been fascinated with the mystical, and this country would provide a gold mine of inspiration. She'd never thought she would get this far at such a young age.

Bridget delivered the eggs and bacon, and Caitlin dug in.

Mary went on. "It's especially nice that your new line will have an old Celtic theme."

Mrs. Abernathy, a quiet, motherly looking woman asked, "Could you show us some of your creations?"

"I'm afraid most of my Celtic jewelry is only at the design phase." Caitlin laid her fork aside to explain. "My older pieces are simpler, mostly fairies and castles and unicorns with crystal horns."

"They sound lovely," said Mrs. Abernathy.

Julian leaned closer to Caitlin and met her gaze steadily. "I would like to see your jewelry, or your sketches . . . whenever you're willing to show them to me."

The flirtatious Englishman was attractive enough, in a blond, sharp-featured way. Around forty, intelligent and sophisticated, Julian would make a nice dinner date. Though he could hardly compete with the mysterious horseman from the night before—Mr. Cloak and Fiery Steed.

Uncomfortable with the memory—it still seemed difficult to believe—she ate her breakfast while Professor Abernathy and Alistair MacDonald reintroduced the topic of stolen artifacts.

"At least Scotland doesn't have too many national treasures lying about that are portable," said Abernathy. "You can't pack Hadrian's Wall or standing stones into your suitcase."

"Aye, but there still is gold about. Gold armor and weapons, buried in those old Celtic cairns, they say," Alistair pointed out. "At least according to legend, there's supposed to be a wealth of gold beneath Black Broch. They say the castle was built atop the largest cairn of all."

"But men dug in the past and never found it," argued his wife.

Bridget hovered in the background. "Or they came up cold and dead."

"I heard there were some deaths connected with the place," Alistair admitted. "Maybe it has a curse, like King Tut's tomb."

"It's far worse than any blathering curse," muttered Bridget.

The mention of the old castle ruins sent a chill up Caitlin's spine. She pushed her plate aside and tried to change the subject. "Is there a mechanic in Droon? My car stalled out near the crossroads last night."

"Your car stalled?" Mary said in surprise. "And how is it that you got home? Surely you didn't walk all that way?"

Caitlin felt her neck grow warm. "Actually, I got a ride."

"From a shepherd?" asked Alistair. "Or someone from the village?"

Caitlin shrugged. "I assume the man lives near the Black Broch area. He didn't tell me his name."

Bridget was staring at her rigidly. "And just what would this man be lookin' like?" asked the housekeeper.

"Mid-thirties, handsome, dark hair. He was riding a black horse."

Alistair laughed. "You came home on horseback?"

Bridget's eyes grew wide. "And ye met him at the crossroads?"

Uh-oh. And what kind of superstitious proclamation was the housekeeper about to make now?

"A horseback ride by the light o' the moon," intoned Bridget, continuing to stare closely at Caitlin. "And handsome as Satan himself, weren't he?"

"Is this man someone you know, Bridget?" Alistair asked as more chills crept up Caitlin's spine.

"No one I know personal, praise the Lord." She nervously twisted the dish towel she'd been holding, and cautioned Caitlin, "Miss Montgomery, you should be puttin' salt around all your doors and windows, and nae going out again at night."

Julian laughed. "Come now, what is this hocus-pocus?"

Bridget continued to speak to Caitlin as if they were alone in the room. "And nae be lookin' out the window at night, neither. God help you, meetin' his eyes is a direct and true invitation."

"Don't scare her with your country myths, Bridget."

"Warning her is a Christian duty, sir. Ah, and she could lose her soul, along with her heart . . ."

"To whom?" asked Julian.

"The curse o' Black Broch. The Guardian. He's been there since time out o' mind."

Alistair MacDonald objected, "But Caitlin's not after gold."

"But he's after *her*," insisted Bridget. "He'll be takin' a lass when he's of a mind to—some o' them always up and disappears. My mother and my mother's mother warned me about him. A guardian he may be, but he's also a divil, a demon lover."

Demon lover.

Bridget's words conjured the memory of a dark, cloaked figure astride a great black horse, its nose blowing flumes of white steam in the mist . . . and Caitlin wondered if she'd be better off if her experience turned out to have been a vision, after all.

She'd already had one experience with a dangerous man, and she wasn't about to court another.

CHAPTER TWO

Droon was a tiny, picturesque village that had once depended upon fishing. Boats still plied the town's harbor, and lobster pots sat on the pier, but the cobblestoned main street featured a brand-new tartan-and-souvenir store, as well as a small art gallery, a historic inn and a fancy tea shop. Caitlin stopped by the last before picking up her car. It being early spring, she had her choice of linen-covered tables. The hostess, an iron-haired middle-aged woman, was very attentive.

"Another wee cup o' tea?" she asked before Caitlin had even finished the first.

"Yes, please. And I'd like a second crumpet, as well."

The jelly-filled, buttery sweet rolls were addictive. As were the shop's mouth-watering shortbread cookies and chocolate-covered *gâteaux*. Taking advantage of the "Land o' Cakes" meant exercising to offset the calories. Perhaps she'd walk in the surrounding hills after she retrieved her car from the mechanic the Mac-Donalds had recommended.

Thinking again about the breakdown made her shift uncomfortably in her seat. She knew her nerves were still bothering her about the incident in California. And with each hour that passed, last night's encounter with the mysterious horseman seemed more and more like a dream—not a nightmare, exactly, but eerie nevertheless. Yet she was certain his rescue had been real. Who was he? Alistair agreed the stranger had to be someone who lived in the vicinity. Demon lovers didn't exist, except in folk superstition and fairy tales.

And art.

Caitlin thought about creating some demon lover jewelry designs to exorcise her feelings. Expressing herself creatively always improved her mood. She pulled out the small sketchbook she always carried and started to doodle a horse's head.

"Ah, now isn't that bonny!" said the shop's hostess, returning with the teapot and another crumpet. "Are you an artist?"

Caitlin nodded and self-consciously shut the sketchbook.

"There was a flock of artists in the village last summer," the hostess prattled. "They weren't a very talented group, in my opinion. Why, one strange lad splashed colors onto his canvas every which way. Said he was painting important landmarks of Scottish history." She snorted. "You should have seen his picture of Black Broch, a muddy mass of black and gray...with streaks of red, probably for blood, o' course."

Caitlin immediately saw the horseman in her mind's eye, the image tainted by the mention of blood. "The ruins above the crossroads?"

"Aye. The scene of many a bloody battle, don't you know. One laird buried a whole regiment alive in a stony pit. They say the screams of the poor trapped souls could be heard for miles."

Caitlin shivered. "A gruesome history."

The hostess nodded. "The lad claimed he even heard the screams himself."

"Probably a bad dream." Caitlin wondered if the artist could be her mystery man. "What did this guy look like?"

"Uh-hmm...short and plain of face. A bit on the stout side."

"Oh." Not her midnight rider.

Before leaving the tea shop, Caitlin asked the hostess if she knew of anyone who matched the mystery man's description. The woman said no. As did the elderly pharmacist who owned the chemist's shop next door.

"You can be certain no one lives in or near that pile of rocks," the pharmacist insisted, adjusting his wire-rimmed spectacles. "Not unless it's Auld Sandy, I suppose, passing through with his flock of sheep."

Caitlin was ready to grasp any possibility. "Auld Sandy?"

"Aye, stay out of his way. The poor soul is crazy." Obviously aware of Caitlin's intense interest, the man explained, "Auld Sandy is half-wild. He's a hermit of sorts. He's lived alone up in the mountains for years with his sheep, and people say he cannot speak English at all anymore. He just *baaa*s."

Caitlin eliminated Auld Sandy from contention.

"Some people say there's only ewes in Sandy's flock, and they follow him for love," the pharmacist went on, taking Caitlin's money and handing her change. "And why not? He probably smells and looks like a sheep himself by now."

Despite herself, Caitlin joined in the elderly man's laughter. "I'll give Auld Sandy a wide berth if I happen to run into him." Though she couldn't say the same for the mysterious rider, who was handsome enough to appeal to any woman, even if he might not attract sheep.

But Caitlin wasn't smiling when she entered the mechanic's place, a new tin-roofed garage that had been built between two stone houses. Jack, the sturdy, bushy-browed, grubby man who'd repaired her car, showed her a thick handful of blackened wires. "Look it this, will ye? Burnt to a crisp. It's a wonder yer engine dinna blow up in flames."

Caitlin frowned. "What causes burned-out wires?"

"A fire in the engine."

"But I didn't see any smoke."

"Tha's wha' I'm tellin' ye," Jack said. "*Twasn't* no fire. The engine is nae damaged at all." He held up the wires again. "So how could this happen?"

Puzzled herself, Caitlin admitted, "You've got me."

The mechanic shook his head and led her to the worktable near the wall. "Wha' a mystery." He gave Caitlin a receipt and she paid him. The car rental agency would reimburse her. "Nearly makes a man believe in fairy fire."

The statement made Caitlin pause and stare. "What?"

"Ah, 'tis nothing but a bairn's tale—ye know, magical flames that burn blue and eat up some things while nae touching others."

Remembering reading about the legend as a child, Caitlin nodded. "The type of fire that doesn't smoke." The appearance of her mystery man had certainly been the stuff from which legends were made. "Say, do you know of anyone who lives near Black Broch—a tall, dark man of about thirty-five or so? He's good-looking, has black hair, rides a black horse."

Jack's reply was decisive. "Sorry, I dinna know anyone who fits tha' particular description." Then he fixed his bushy gaze on her. "Wha' were ye doing about

Black Broch, anyway? MacDonald said yer car up and
died there in the middle of the night. Sometimes there
be smugglers about, even in this modern day.''

"Smugglers?"

"Aye, men who bring in goods by sea. Desperate,
dangerous men. Ye should be careful.''

And with that abrupt pronouncement, Jack left her
to take care of another customer who had entered the
garage.

Dissatisfied with all she'd heard of Black Broch and
the explanations of who her mystery man might be,
Caitlin drove out of town. Instead of stopping somewhere near her bed-and-breakfast, she found herself
heading directly for the crossroads. Though nobody
seemed to know the midnight rider, she was drawn to
the site of their encounter, her fascination nearly mor-
bid after all the tales of bloody battles and smugglers
she'd heard.

Besides, she rationalized, she had her Demon Lover
designs to work on and where better than in this at-
mospheric place.

Hoping she wasn't tempting fate, she pulled over on
the road where she'd left the car the night before. Frozen in her seat for a moment, she stared out the window at the cairns nearby, then at the ruins of the aged
castle on the promontory above—dark stones that
brooded against the clear blue afternoon sky.

Black Broch put her on her guard, even while drawing her closer.

Climbing the steep hill would certainly be good exercise, and she was thankful she'd worn walking shoes
with her casual sweater and pants. She locked her purse
in the trunk, took her sketchbook and set off. She was

nearly out of breath by the time she reached the top of the promontory, and she paused to lean against a fallen stone. Glancing up, she noticed a falcon coasting on the updrafts high overhead. The bird dipped its wings and drifted lower.

Black Broch was larger than it looked from the road, Caitlin discovered as she explored. And as forbidding up close as its reputation. Only parts of the structure were still intact. Near the edge of the cliff overlooking the sea loch, a couple of towers stood tall and solid, their narrow slits of windows once meant to protect the inhabitants from enemy arrows. Castellated walls that had crumbled in places connected the towers and surrounded a weedy inner courtyard.

Caitlin approached an arched opening that led into the stone-paved courtyard. Her pulse quickened as she peered about. A salt-laden wind gusted off the sea, soughing about the old castle with near-human moans. Goose bumps rose on her neck, and she glanced around furtively. She'd only have Auld Sandy or smugglers to deal with at the worst, she told herself, and the latter surely wouldn't be about in broad daylight.

Though she might have a problem with a territorial bird. The falcon Caitlin had seen earlier suddenly swooped low, shrieking so loudly she ducked into the courtyard for fear the bird intended to attack.

"Crazy featherhead!" she yelled. The talons of a bird of prey could really do some damage. Thank goodness, the bird took off again.

She looked around the more protected courtyard, which was colder and spookier up close. Caitlin hugged herself, wishing she'd brought her coat. Sunlight never reached some of these dark shadows. They were as cold and forbidding as they'd probably been when the castle was built.

She knew that on this same site, a fortified tower, or broch, had existed in the time of the early Celts. Caitlin wondered about the Celtic cairn that was supposed to lie beneath the castle's foundations. Had the castle's medieval builders ever dug down into it? Was that the same place where the evil laird had buried the soldiers? And where was the dungeon? Castles always had dungeons.

Trying not to spook herself with such musings, she peered closely at the walls as she wandered along. When some faint carvings attracted her eye, she scratched away dead vines to find a line of runes.

"Incredible!"

Awed by the realization that the hand of another human had created the magical symbols thousands of years before, she forgot her unfounded fears and opened her sketchbook to draw. But first, she lightly ran her fingers over the marks, hoping their power had been meant to do good, not evil.

"Trespassers! Invaders! Attack, attack! Take up yer sword!"

Having been deeply and soundly asleep, Bain Morghue groaned as Ghillie Brown shook him until his teeth rattled.

"I tell ye, there be an enemy about! Take up yer sword!" screeched the old man.

Bain opened a hostile eye, ready to throttle his servant, but then the meaning of Ghillie's words suddenly sank in. In one smooth movement, adrenaline surging, he rolled his long body out of the great four-poster and wrapped his plaid about him.

Ghillie handed him the claymore and scabbard that had been hanging on the headboard. The stones on the pommel caught the light as Bain withdrew the deadly length of steel.

"Enemies? Where?" he demanded.

"In the courtyard! In the courtyard!" Ghillie squealed, nearly doing a little dance in his desperate excitement. "They be seeking a way to get in and kill us both!"

Forever worried that intruders could mean the end of him, Bain hurried toward the steps that led up to the main entrance, his bare feet slapping on the cold stone. Reaching into a crevice at the landing, he cracked open the great door and slipped out quickly before it closed behind him.

Sword drawn, he prepared to shout a war cry as he hurtled into the courtyard. The sound died in his throat when he saw who whipped about to stare at him, her big green eyes round, her face ghost-white against the red of her hair. He was hit hard, his immediate response physical, the same response he'd experienced upon seeing her the first time. No matter. He didn't know her or her connections. She could be a thief. Or worse. She didn't belong here.

"And what is it you're up to, wandering about where you're not wanted?" A few more strides brought him towering over her. He shoved her hard against the wall. She made a choked sound and dropped the tablet she was carrying. It took all his will to ignore her softness. To steel himself against her alluring woman-scent. "I didn't give you leave to set foot on my property," he went on in his most intimidating tone. "I could kill you where you stand!"

Her eyes grew wider. "K-kill me?"

Though he could think of a thousand things he would rather do to her—with her—Bain kept himself in check. "You do understand the word *kill*, do you not, lady?" For good measure, he brandished the claymore in her face. "Now... what are you doing on my property?"

She stared at him, speechless but defiant.

He tightened his strong grip on her arm until she cried out, growing frantic. Struggling, she yelled, "Let go of me!"

"Orders?" he asked, his voice purposely soft and menacing. "I should be more accommodating if I were you, lady." He wondered if she'd been sent to test his defenses.

Wild to get away, she struggled futilely against his greater strength, and at last managed to stomp on his bare foot.

"Ahh!" His face contorted in pain, but he didn't release her. "You little vixen!"

She tried to stomp his foot again, but he grabbed her other arm and pushed her back, looming over her so close that her panting breath feathered his face. His groin tightened, and he was tempted to kiss her. To let his long-unassuaged lust consume them both. Then, perhaps, she would give him the satisfaction of seeing her quake.

She had the audacity to glare at him. "I didn't do anything wrong!"

"You're trespassing. 'Tis a crime."

"Then call the authorities and leave me be! You're nothing but a bully."

"You dare reproach me?"

"I'd dare more if I could!"

Surprised by and respectful of her grit, deciding that perhaps he had made a mistake and that she was no threat after all, he laughed and let go. Off balance, she stumbled backward, smacking her head hard against the stone wall. Her lashes fluttered, and her knees gave way.

Bain caught her before she fell. "Silly, nervy lass," he growled, raking a hand through her hair and coming up with a smear of blood. "Now look what you've done."

Look what *she'd* done?

Caitlin's heart ricocheted in her chest from immediate fear, and from something she couldn't quite define...something that went deeper...and was infinitely more dangerous. But she was too weak to object when he picked her up and carried her out of the courtyard into the wan afternoon sunlight. Her head was throbbing. She ignored the pain, and the lump that lodged squarely in her throat, and the little thrill that the proximity to his naked flesh gave her. She moaned and closed her eyes.

A minute later, she opened them again to find they'd entered a cool, dark passage. The horseman was descending. She would never have imagined the man to appear, wild-haired and half-naked in a trailing plaid, brandishing a sword. She would never have imagined being carried off by him. At the bottom of the steps, light beckoned from an open door.

"Ghillie!" he roared, so loud that her head throbbed even worse.

"Can you tone it down, please?" she whispered weakly.

He paid no attention and yelled again, then brought Caitlin into a firelit room to lay her across a cushioned, thronelike chair. She wasn't sure if the place actually resembled a medieval reception hall—fireplace, sconces filled with candles, high rafters and tapestries—or if she was delirious.

She thought she must be hallucinating for sure when the person named Ghillie appeared. He was a very short, ugly man with weathered, leathery skin that was nearly the same brown color as his clothing. Although bald, Ghillie had tufts of hair growing from the tops of his huge ears that made him look shaggy. She blinked into his beady little eyes and groaned.

"Get hot water and a clean rag," the rider ordered. "The lady has hurt her head."

Ghillie seemed reluctant. "But, Laird—"

Laird? Her midnight rider was a nobleman?

"No buts. Go fetch what I ask for. She is not our enemy."

Muttering to himself, the strange brown man skittered away.

Caitlin leaned back against the cushions and once more closed her eyes. And prayed... If only she could get out of the place unscathed... She'd had enough experiences with this threatening, if fascinating, man.

When the throbbing quieted, she opened her eyes. Ghillie was staring down at her, basin and rag in hand. He wrinkled his bulbous nose as if in distaste. Masking her fear once more, Caitlin glared at him and quickly sat up. Ghillie croaked and jumped back, water sloshing. Despite having been told she meant no harm, he was obviously as afraid of her as she was of him.

Surprised, she felt stronger for the knowledge. "Where did the hulk go?"

Ghillie wiggled his bushy brows. "Who? Who? Laird Morghue?"

"Morghue? Is that his name?"

"The laird be changin' his clothing."

"Good idea. It's too cold to be wearing nothing but a bolt of fabric." Though she admitted Morghue had been quite an eyeful. Since Ghillie continued to stand like an unmoving rock, Caitlin reached for the basin and rag. "Can I have those?"

He surrendered the items gladly and scurried away.

She winced when she touched the back of her head and felt the rising, egg-sized lump. Putting the basin on the stone floor, she immersed the rag in the hot water, wrung it out and started to clean her wound.

Strong fingers clasped hers. "Allow me. You cannot see what you are doing."

Her muscles froze, and she had to force her arms down. She couldn't relax, not remembering how he'd talked of killing her with the fancy sword with the gold hilt and jeweled pommel. He came around to the front of her chair. Reluctantly she noted that he looked almost as good in the black trousers, shirt and boots as he had without them. Expressionless, he knelt and gently swabbed the lump, holding her jaw steady. She tried not to flinch in reaction to the tingling warmth of his touch.

Even so, she couldn't help but mutter, "Haven't you done enough to me already?"

"You hit your head yourself, lass. It wasn't I who did the damage. Besides, you were trespassing."

"If you're so uptight about someone coming onto your property, you ought to put up fences and signs." She paused, thinking about the inquiries she'd made in Droon. "Incidentally, nobody seems to know this castle *is* your property. They don't even know who *you* are."

He didn't respond. Turning her face directly toward him, he gazed so deeply into her eyes that she caught her breath and all thought fled. For a moment, she was lost....

"Your pupils seem normal."

His observation broke the spell, and she squirmed a little and cleared her throat. "At least I don't have a concussion."

He rose, towering over her. "So you can be on your way."

Oddly enough, she was dismayed. Only moments ago, she had prayed to escape unscathed. And now that she had permission, she was reluctant to run. She wanted to see more of the fascinating place... and of Morghue. He was dangerous, yes. Maybe that was part of his fascination. That, and a seething virility she couldn't deny, made former boyfriend Neil Howard pale by comparison. Thinking of how badly that short-lived attraction had turned out—Neil had ended up threatening and stalking her—Caitlin wondered whether she was drawn to the wrong sort of man.

If he'd really meant to hurt her, Caitlin told herself, he would have done so, instead of taking care of her injury. If she was cautious, she should be safe enough for a while longer.

She licked her parched lips and once more ignored her good sense, which told her to run while she had the chance. "The last time we met, I believe you said I could see you if I wanted to."

"And so you have."

"But now you're kicking me out?"

"I respect your courage and am giving you your freedom, lady. There's a difference."

He said it so seriously, she once more had to tamp down her alarm. "So, what—you were considering locking me in your dungeon?" She couldn't help herself. "Who do you think you are, some medieval over-lord?"

"I know who I am, as do my enemies who seek me."

She frowned and muttered, "Sounds like a fairy tale to me."

"Fairy tale! Fairy tale!" muttered Ghillie in the background. Caitlin hadn't realized he was lurking nearby.

She glanced toward the sound as he opened the shutters of a high, narrow window. A large bird flapped inside and sank its talons into a leather-covered perch near the wall.

Again wondering if she was dreaming, Caitlin murmured, "A hunting falcon? I guess you do live like a medieval lord. Not that that gives you the right to be so high-handed. Furthermore, as far as seeking you out is concerned, I've been asking around about you, and I've yet to find out your full name."

"'Tis Bain Morghue."

Finally. "Laird Morghue?"

"Bain will do," he said.

"I'm Caitlin Montgomery as I stated before."

"Fine, brave Caitlin, and now that we've taken care of the niceties, I fear I must encourage you to leave again. It will soon be dark outside."

The more he tried to get rid of her, the more she felt like digging in. Who gave him the right to push her around? They didn't live in feudal times.

"I'm not afraid of the dark." Not normally. She glanced at the heavy wooden table on one side of the fireplace. A flask of amber liquid glimmered there, surrounded by several goblets. Her mouth was so dry, she could barely swallow. "I could use a drink before I leave. Is that brandy? Sherry?"

"Neither." Bain's tone was clipped. "You wouldn't care for it."

"A sip or two would soothe my headache, get my blood pumping again." And give her a little time to find out more about this mysterious man and his castle. She wanted answers. And she wanted to dispel the notion that she lacked solid judgment when it came to men. When Bain didn't make a move, she said, "Surely you owe me one gesture of hospitality."

He gazed at her measuringly.

And, unexpectedly, he broke the fine thread of tension between them by laughing. "All right then, I see how it is." His voice mellowed to a smooth and rather seductive tone, making Caitlin's toes tingle and her senses go on alert. "You shall get what you want, fair lass." He turned to the man who seemed to be his servant. "Ghillie, pour us out two goblets."

"But—But—" the brown man huffed.

Bain merely stared imperiously until Ghillie did as he was told. Then he dragged a chair up close to Caitlin's. Ghillie brought the drinks on a pewter tray. As Caitlin reached for hers, the brown man looked directly at her, eyes wide.

"Is it poison or something?" she asked, her hand hovering.

"Of course not, or it would also kill me," Bain assured her. When she finally took her drink, he motioned Ghillie away. "It's only my own specially distilled liqueur."

She stared into the goblet—old-fashioned handblown glass in which the substance seemed to glow. Smiling, Bain lightly clicked the rim of his goblet against Caitlin's before taking a sip. She hesitated—for who knew what dangers lurked in the goblet—then told herself that if he could drink the stuff, she certainly could. She took a tiny sip. The liqueur was soothing, smooth, slightly sweet, yet light—and most definitely alcoholic. Perhaps it was her mood or her injury, but the mere taste of the stuff went directly to her head.

Indeed, her pain already receding, Caitlin took a bigger sip and watched the room pulse with warmth. "It makes me feel a lot better."

"I'm sure you would feel nice anyway."

Titillated, she noted the flickering of the torches, reflected in his intense eyes. For a moment, their blue nearly seemed a shade of violet.

"You can stay here all night if you wish, lass."

Startled, Caitlin sat up straighter and felt the blood creep up her neck. He certainly wasn't implying she could curl up by herself in front of the fire. "I only wanted a drink, not a proposition." Though she had to admit she found the idea oddly intriguing, considering the fact that the man had given her such a fright.

His expression knowing, he crooked a rakish eyebrow at her. "Sometimes you receive more than you bargain for."

The reminder brought her back to her senses. "You're very attractive, Mr. Bain Morghue, but awfully full of yourself. We've barely met." Feeling his very presence bearing down on her, she tried to keep things light. "And I'd have to know more about you and this situation before I even agreed to be friends."

"Sometimes there are no easy explanations."

"Try me." Realizing he could take that the wrong way, she immediately rushed on, "I mean, tell me how you managed to obtain this property without any of your neighbors knowing about it."

His smile appeared almost demonic as he slid a hand along the arm of his chair, until their fingers were mere centimeters apart. Her pulse surged. She yearned to be touched—the urge was so strong that she was shocked at herself—but somehow she managed to slip her own hand onto her lap.

"You *do* own this castle, don't you?"

He leaned forward. "Aye."

Nervously she inched farther back in her seat and glanced at the nearest tapestry, which showed a herd of does fleeing a hunter. "So, did you, uh...buy this place recently?"

His look seared her. "I've owned it since time out of mind."

Time out of mind? Hadn't she heard that phrase before? She couldn't quite remember where or when, as she considered the subject of deeds in the British Isles. Perhaps they could stretch back a very long time.

"Are you saying you inherited this castle? Then how come no one in Droon knows that? Why hasn't anyone heard of you?" She held up a cautioning hand, partly to keep him at bay. "And don't give me some answer about how people who seek you will know you, and so on." When he didn't answer, merely stared at her as if he were looking inside her, she prompted him. "Surely there's an explanation that makes sense.... Maybe you've been an absentee landlord for years."

"That is true," he finally said. "I have other, similar holdings in Scotland, as well as in Ireland and Wales, that have taken my time."

"Castles? And why have you come back here?" She glanced about. "Are you fixing up the place? It'd make a great tourist attraction. Maybe even an inn of sorts. You must be wealthy."

"I have gold beyond measure."

"Gold? Now that *has* to be an exaggeration. No one hoards gold these days." Although he would indeed need big bucks to go around fixing up castles.

"All right, stocks, bonds, whatever you wish to call it." Then she caught her breath when he reached over to brush back a tendril of her hair. "Red is a bonny color."

Face warm, she stirred in her seat and tried to forget about how handsome and mesmerizing he was. And how centered. She hadn't gotten his mind steered in another direction, after all. She reminded herself he might be dangerous on every level and that she therefore couldn't let down her guard. Glancing at the tapestry, she saw there was actually only one doe in the design, not a herd, and that the hunter seemed closer than she'd thought originally. She shifted uncomfortably—her mind was fuzzy with liqueur.

But not fuzzy enough to let him continue playing with her hair. She knew where that would lead. She brushed his hand away and tried to distract him once more.

"So why hasn't anyone around here heard of you? Do you own Black Broch under a corporate name or something?"

"You are a very clever and lovely lady."

He grasped her hand, giving it a squeeze that alarmed her even as it sent little thrills of pleasure zinging up her arm. He drew her closer, yet didn't really pull.

She squirmed. It would be so easy to give in. His gaze was hypnotic....

Giving in would be a mistake, perhaps the biggest of her life. "So what's the name of this corporation?" she croaked.

He frowned, let go of her hand and, for the first time, leaned away from her, back into his chair. "I grow tired of this interrogation. I have my reasons to keep my own counsel."

Relieved that he'd put some distance between them, she hazarded a guess. "Real estate rivals?"

"Rivals?" He nodded. "There are those who would plot against me. For your own sake, keep your visit here secret."

"*My* sake?"

"Most would not believe you, anyway. But enough." He leaned forward again, and when he next spoke his tone was silky. "Now 'tis your turn. What are you really doing here?"

She knew he meant this very place, this very moment, and she was certain he'd like her to admit she was besotted with him and longed to jump into his bed. Her heart raced, and her insides quaked with an even more encompassing kind of fear than she'd experienced earlier.

"I thought this castle would provide inspiration for my new jewelry collection. I'm an artist."

He stared at her thoughtfully. "Hmm...someone who sees beyond this world. Is that why you've asked for me, sought me out so diligently?"

Was he suggesting that he himself was not of the ordinary world? "I want to do some designs that are based on the myth of the demon lover," she said, drawing on Bridget's fantastic tale. "You'd fit the role quite nicely—romantically handsome, powerful persona, mysterious, an air of danger."

His momentary surprise turned to laughter. "Only an *air* of danger?" He leaned even farther forward to graze her cheek with a lazy finger before he took firm hold of her jaw. "Then it's off to my lair, lass, to prove I'm truly dangerous. I'll sample that fair, soft skin all of a piece."

She felt as if she were being zapped with raw electricity. Was he going to kiss her? She'd be lost for sure. Intuitively knowing that, if she allowed it, he could dominate her at some primal level she wanted to keep within her own control, she pulled away and rose from her chair, her limbs lethargic from too much sitting and strong alcohol. Still, fear of any kind was sobering.

"You are absolutely incredible. You ought to be an actor."

He rose, as well. "You think my words part of an act?" Then he took hold of her shoulders and drew her tightly against him, belly against belly, thigh against thigh. Her breasts flattened against his chest. "Is what you're feeling not real?" He smiled and angled his head as if to take her mouth. "A demon lover is what you seek, eh? Then beware, fair Caitlin, for once you find him, running will do you no good. He will have power over you, even in the dark."

Desperately she turned her face and pushed against him. "Let go! I don't need to run. I already told you I'm not afraid of the dark."

"You *are* very courageous."

She looked at him defiantly, thinking of her younger brother, who had been traumatized so terribly as a child, he'd retreated from reality. "I've fought the darkness and won. Gone into the deep night of the mind and brought back someone I loved...and I know I could do it again."

He frowned, and his hold loosened. "You must be very powerful."

"My love was powerful. That's all the magic I needed."

Though her adult, professional fascination with spells and fairy tales and crystals had begun when her little brother was lost inside himself, her work had grown from beliefs that were mostly left behind with childhood.

"Heart and willpower. You are blessed with both." He allowed her to step away. "All right, Caitlin Montgomery, you may do as you wish—go or stay."

"I'm leaving." While she had the chance, and before he got her to reveal other secrets, which wouldn't make her look so strong after all. Relieved at a deep, if inarticulate, level, she glanced at her watch. It still showed five o'clock. "My watch must have stopped."

"The door is this way," Bain told her, walking away.

She followed him out of the firelit room, into a long passageway and up a flight of stone steps. What should she say when they parted? What if she never saw him again? She was contemplating the latter question when he opened the door.

"Good night, Caitlin."

The same salty wind was blowing, but the afternoon had turned to twilight—the gloaming, the Scots called it.

Caitlin turned and stared at Bain for a moment until he raised her hand and kissed it, turning it over to likewise set his lips softly against the palm. Her skin reacted to the light brush, and she backed away.

"I shall dream of you if we don't meet again," he told her, retreating inside.

Not meeting him again—that was one thing she feared.

And, yes, she still feared *him* also.

The door shut.

And the thought made her heart ache. "Why won't I see you? Are you leaving for one of your other sites?" she called. But if he heard, he made no response.

Mysterious, reclusive man.

And not-too-bright woman, she told herself, glancing about. *Escape while you can!* But she didn't have a flashlight, or even a match, to show her the way down the steep, dark hillside.

And Bain Morghue had candles.

Glancing up at the tower she'd just left, she moved forward to knock, surprised when she couldn't make out the shape of a door. Where was it? She hadn't so much as taken two steps away. Circling the tower didn't help, either. She finally concluded that the door must have been the trick kind, similar to those that swung out to reveal secret chambers.

She was tired, injured, and still a tiny bit tipsy from the strong and unusual liqueur. The latter was probably the reason the rocks and bits of heather looked so beautiful as she meandered down the side of the promontory. Even the sound of the waves on the loch sounded like high, sweet, beckoning voices.

Everything seemed more intense because of the intoxicating drink—no doubt the reason she'd responded to Bain the way she had. For no matter how handsome he was, or how appealing he appeared to be, Bain Morghue was a dangerous man, one who would be reckoned with on his own terms.

Thank God she had escaped his lair unscathed this time.

Hidden behind one of the larger stones in the cairns below Black Broch, he watched Caitlin Montgomery descend slowly, get into her car and drive off.

Strange.

He hadn't considered her a potential opponent.

All that prattle about designing jewelry. All that innocent, fresh-faced interest in the beauty of Scotland. All that surprise over the stalled car and the midnight ride.

He was usually astute, but he had believed her, thought her authentic.

Of course, there was another possible explanation for the American woman's entry into the castle today. A simple explanation. His enemy had rightfully earned his reputation as a womanizer par excellence.

He fingered the sketchbook he'd managed to pick up in the small courtyard—closer than he'd ever gotten before. He'd opened the pages and seen her amateur attempt at drawing the old runes. If she *was* a rival, she had hardly reached his own level of expertise. And she could be quite useful. Hadn't she kept his enemy so busy that the bastard had not been aware of the threat so close to his inner abode? Even the sharp-eyed sentry hadn't detected his presence.

Rising, he stared up at the dark castle, wondering if he should use her or rid himself of possible competition. It would take some serious thought. In the end, he would utilize every weapon, take every measure, use every ounce of strength necessary, to get what he wanted.

Soon.

CHAPTER THREE

"My wife and I are going to Lochfynton to see the standing stones tomorrow morning," Professor Abernathy told Caitlin early the next evening in the parlor, where everyone had gathered for the traditional before-dinner sherry. He took a sip. "We thought you might like to join us."

Though she didn't need alcohol after being so tipsy the day before, that she'd gone to bed without dinner and slept fourteen hours, Caitlin politely tried her own drink. The sherry wasn't nearly as tasty—or as heady—as Bain's brew. But then, dangerous or not, Bain Morghue was heady enough for any red-blooded woman. He seemed to seethe with seductiveness and power.

Suddenly realizing that the professor was waiting for her answer, Caitlin snapped back to the present. *The standing stones.* She had been looking forward to seeing the local monoliths, similar to those at Stonehenge.

"How kind of you to offer," she said graciously. "You're sure I won't be intruding?"

"No, no, not at all. Mrs. Abernathy and I want to get to know you better." The professor leaned in a little closer. "It'll be nice to spend time with another American. Sometimes I have to fight through the native accent to comprehend what's being said," he admitted.

"I understand completely," she murmured, distracted by bits of images and sounds that flitted through her mind.

No matter how hard she tried, she couldn't close herself off from her encounter with Bain, and that fact disturbed her deeply. But surely she could handle the Scotsman, after her experience with Neil, her troubled ex-boyfriend. For one, it had taken several dates for her to recognize Neil's dark side, while she'd recognized the darkness in Bain straight off. Forewarned was forearmed, right?

"Professor. Caitlin." Julian joined them, looking at Caitlin with great interest. "We seem to have missed each other yesterday evening, and you didn't join us for breakfast this morning. You must have made some exciting finds."

"Not that exciting."

At least not today, when she'd taken what she'd hoped would be a mind- and spirit-cleansing walk about the countryside. Instead, she'd dwelled on Bain. And for some reason—no doubt due to the warning he'd given her—she was hesitant about mentioning her encounter with Bain to anyone. That she felt as if he had a hold over her made her distinctly uneasy.

"I saw your car parked in the driveway," Julian said as Alistair and Mary and the professor's wife joined them, glasses in hand. "A new model. What was wrong with it, anyway?"

"The mechanic wasn't certain," Caitlin said. "Some mysterious burned-out wires. All he could suggest was fairy fire."

Julian started, while Alistair laughed and said, "Quite the imaginative one, that Jack."

"May the dear Lord protect us!" Bridget stood frozen, halfway to putting away the sherry decanter, a beautiful piece of cut crystal with a stopper in the shape of a fairy. "Ye shouldna laugh at what ye nae ken, Mr. MacDonald."

"Now, Bridget," admonished Mary kindly, "there are no fairies. Jacko is full of stories, is all."

Bridget shook her head in disagreement and replaced the decanter in the liquor cabinet, then swept out of the room, mumbling ominously to herself.

"Fairy fire? Is that some kind of local legend?" asked Mrs. Abernathy.

"No, not local." Mary was clearly warming to the topic. "All of Scotland is riddled with legends. Our sherry decanter pays tribute to the tale of fairy wine, you know."

"Fairy wine?" Caitlin echoed faintly.

"A magical brew that's said to intensify the senses," Mary went on. "To make things more beautiful or more frightening. Of course, legend has it that any potion or food a mortal takes from a fairy has the power to bind that person to its magical giver forever, unless the giver chooses to release the person."

The others smiled and laughed at the idea. But not Caitlin.

Uneasily, she remembered how, after drinking Bain's brew, all her senses had seemed more alert, how her fright had multiplied . . . and her longings. And it was true, she'd spent far too much time thinking of Bain. But *fairy wine?*

"Speaking of legends," Alistair said, "some friends of ours would like to meet you, Caitlin. They're interested in seeing your jewelry designs, and they're willing to share their knowledge of Celtic myths, a particular interest of theirs. Perhaps tomorrow afternoon?''

"All right.'' Caitlin couldn't pass up such a terrific opportunity. And she had to admit she wouldn't mind some company, so that she could get over this growing obsession with a man she would probably never see again. Thinking about him wasn't good for her at all. "I appreciate all the help I can get.''

"Sounds like you're going to have a full day tomorrow.'' Julian moved closer, as if determined to be the focus of her attention. "Have you had the chance yet to explore Droon?''

"I drove around town after I picked up my car yesterday.''

"Then took the road out along the coast?''

"Actually, I followed it all the way to Black Broch. That old castle is really a fascinating place.''

The firelit tête-à-tête came back to her with goose-flesh-inducing clarity. The way Bain Morghue's touch had made her bones melt. The way his eyes had devoured her. The way his threat to sample her all of a piece had aroused as much as frightened her. She told herself she should try to learn more about the mysterious man. Surely if he really was the Morghue, a Scottish laird, the MacDonalds would know of him. And some reality-sharing would make her feel safer.

Bain had insisted that people would not believe her, she remembered, had warned that she should keep quiet for her own sake. His other warning, his reference to rivals, kept her tongue in check. She would not leak out Bain Morghue's presence. In her mind, what were probably real estate rivals had become enemies, and at some level, she felt as if his enemies were *her* enemies. A ridiculous idea—after all, she didn't even *know* the man—and yet one she couldn't shake. In some strange, indefinable way, she felt a connection to him, despite his threats.

"Black Broch?" Julian mused, his brow furrowed. "You ought to avoid that place. Today I heard a convict is loose in the vicinity. Supposedly a dangerous, desperate man. If he's hiding amidst the rubble of Black Broch, you could have put yourself in danger, wandering around alone."

A convict loose. A dangerous, desperate man. Bain? A chill shot through Caitlin. The description certainly matched.

"Don't worry, I'm always careful."

But how safe was a woman when faced with a near-naked man brandishing a claymore—and, worse, a mesmerizing quality that made him unforgettable?

The gloaming. Twilight. Barely forty-eight hours after her second encounter with the most fascinating man she'd ever met, Caitlin stood in a circle of standing stones that loomed over her like rugged, if inanimate, giants, and replayed their meeting in her mind.

And wondered if they would meet again. She knew she should hope they wouldn't.

She'd dreamed of him the night before. Whether asleep or awake, she remembered every detail of Bain Morghue. Dark hair, perpetually windblown. Chiseled features. Strong yet gentle fingers. Blue eyes nearly violet. Seething virility. Too bad he'd frightened her so, she hadn't been able to properly appreciate his appearing before her in nothing but a plaid. Now she longed for another look, the chance to see whether her memory betrayed her or he really had the most beautiful male form she'd ever seen.

Caitlin sighed, both wishing for and dreading another encounter with her mysterious midnight rider. Was she really attracted to the wrong sort of man?

A day that should have been stimulating had quickly grown flat. After remembering that she'd left a nearly full sketchbook lying amid the damp stones of Black Broch, she'd swallowed her frustration and come here to the windswept area near Lochfynton this morning with Professor and Mrs. Abernathy. The couple had been so happy to talk to another American that they'd never stopped. Another sketchbook in hand, she hadn't been able to draw the ancient Celtic patterns decorating the standing stones.

That afternoon, the MacDonalds and their friends, the Fergusons, had been so interested in seeing her designs and in finding out about her plans for the research trip that they'd barely mentioned the Guardian of Black Broch before cutting short their discussion of Celtic myth. Of course, they'd promised to make it up to her another day.

And afterward, she'd suffered through an incredibly boring early-evening tea. Julian Taylor had caught her going into the tea shop and insisted on joining her. Though he was good-looking and ostensibly charming, he'd talked about antiques until Caitlin had wished she'd never heard of the subject.

Or maybe it was just that she'd met Bain Morghue, after whom all other men would seem boring.

She certainly was popular with the people at the B-and-B, and especially with Julian, who had asked to see her again. She'd been ready to turn him down, but then she'd thought better of it. He was nothing like Bain Morghue and she wanted to prove something to herself about the men she chose to see.

Though, at the moment, she greatly appreciated being alone.

But was she?

A scuffling of gravel made her whip around, staring off toward the darkening path that led to her car. No one in sight. Probably some small animal. She tamped down the slight thrill that shot through her...the memory that threatened to panic her.

Caitlin told herself to stop imagining things. The standing stones were the reason she was there, and soon it would be too chill and dark for her to accomplish anything.

She closed her eyes and tried to imagine what it might have been like to be part of this corner of the world three thousand years before. The Bronze Age. No modern conveniences. Only the earth and its riches on which to rely. The wind swept eerily through the circle of rugged stones set on end by a primitive people who had used them for religious or astronomical or agricultural purposes.

The gods worshipped by Bronze Age people had eventually come to be called the elder race...or the fairy folk, if one wanted to be even more whimsical.

Fairy folk... fairy fire... fairy wine.

Caitlin shivered.

The Scottish mist was laving her upturned face. She opened her eyes. The weather was turning, and she hadn't yet gotten one sketch. Determined to accomplish something before she was forced to leave, she opened her notebook and drew closer to one of the stones, which was irregular in width, craggy at the top. While several of the others were decorated with the simpler and more common cup-and-ring markings of the Bronze Age, this one was covered with a more intricate design—lozenges, chevrons and triangles had been incised or pecked in a number of combinations over most of the surface that was turned toward the ring's center.

Sketching quickly, Caitlin was busily filling the page when her sense of unease returned twofold. The back of her neck prickled. Her pencil hovered over the paper. Her heart thumped strongly in her chest. Neither noise nor movement betrayed another presence, yet she was certain she wasn't alone, as if her sixth sense had been finely honed somehow....

No fool she, Caitlin closed her notebook with the casual air of someone who had finished her business. She backed off and looked around, her manner innocuous but her gaze intent. Nothing. Yet the instinctual warning didn't fade. She'd had no such warning the night Neil Howard was waiting for her outside her apartment building. Still keeping her composure, she stuffed her notebook into her shoulder bag—she wasn't about to lose another one—and headed for the path to her car.

It was only when her sneakered foot touched gravel that she more than sensed another presence. The sounds of rustling clothing and furtive footfalls seemed magnified to her ears. And from the corner of her eye she caught a dark blur to her left, traversing the narrow opening between two of the standing stones.

Dark, but not familiar. A man, but not Bain, she told herself. Someone who'd been sneaking around and spying on her.

Her stride lengthened, and she had her keys in hand even before she got to the car. She was locked inside in seconds, and was driving away from the ancient site in less than a minute. Her arms were tense, and her fingers stiff around the wheel. Her eyes kept darting to the rearview mirror as the sky turned a threatening charcoal gray.

The mist thickened, casting droplets of water against her windshield. Taking a broad curve a tad too fast, Caitlin slowed and turned on the headlights, the wipers, the radio. Maybe some music would help her relax.

She took a deep breath and settled back into the seat, humming along with the classical piece, which she recognized though couldn't name. Her heartbeat steadied, her stomach settled. She'd just about convinced herself she'd been imagining things when another set of headlights swung behind hers as they, too, rounded the curve. But from where? She hadn't passed any buildings. Or any crossroads. The other car must have come from behind some outcropping along the road, near the standing stones.

Caitlin's pulse accelerated and her foot grew heavy on the gas pedal, making the small car accelerate, as well. The headlights behind her fell back, and she knew a moment's relief. But seconds later, the other car regained the lost distance.

Her instincts had been correct all along.

They were warning her now—the person following meant her no good.

She sped along the winding, narrow road too fast for even a clear day. And this was Scotland at its most threatening. Dark and dangerous. Like Bain.

For an instant, she wondered if the man following her *could* be the mysterious laird himself, giving her yet another scare. But no, this was too stealthy an approach for the likes of him. He leaned toward the theatrical. No doubt he would prefer to ride his hellish steed down on her, claymore drawn and raised in threat.

And somehow, if it was Bain, she was certain she would know.

Thunder rumbled overhead and lightning split the sky, for a moment illuminating the road before her. Caitlin's stomach dropped as the car nosed down through the curtain of rain and fog. She was starting the treacherous drive along the sea loch, a section of the road too narrow for two cars to pass each other. She'd been told that cars traveling south backed up to the occasional gravel-covered shoulder to let a northbound vehicle go by. Pray God there was no oncoming traffic this evening!

She checked the rearview mirror again. The headlights were closing in on her, sliding to her left. Was the crazed person really going to try to go around her? Impossible. She would be pushed off the road. And the drop to her right was so steep that the mere thought of it kick-started her heart.

She had no choice.

As dangerous as it was, she threw caution to the winds, pressed the accelerator and prayed she would keep to the curves and not drive straight into the sea.

Some higher power had to be with her, for as distracted as she was by the danger of the elements, in addition to the person behind her, Caitlin kept her little rental car on all four wheels and seemed to know where each hairpin curve lay before reaching it. She safely made it around nearly a dozen curves before the road straightened and widened once more. The fog and rain were so heavy that she couldn't see the drop, but she remembered that the road veered away from the sea here, the shoulder flattening to gravel and grass.

Safe, thank God! Her eyes flashed to the rearview mirror.

The other car made it through, as well.

Caitlin didn't slow for a second. Her mind whirled. What now? How to ditch the maniac? What if he was the crazed convict someone had told Julian about? What if he followed her to the MacDonalds' place?

She would just have to outdrive him, disappear into the mist so that he couldn't find her.

Instinctively she drove straight for the crossroads, her accelerator flattened to the car's floor. Within seconds, it seemed, she had lost the lights behind her. If only she could keep up the pace! Her eyes flicked to the rear-view mirror again and again. No other car. But she wouldn't relax, wouldn't believe that he wasn't there. He was ready to pounce, somewhere behind her. . . .

Approaching the crossroads, she felt her first breath of relief, and only then began to slow down. She had to, in case someone was coming from another direction.

Then lightning lit the sky, revealing the crumbling old tower that stood sentry above the crossroads. The air crackled and boomed, and another streak of white heat found its target in an ancient tree standing next to the road. A loud crack, and then a major limb separated from the trunk and descended before her as she practically stood on the brake to avoid a collision. She fought to keep her car in control as it swerved and twisted and bucked. Below her, the earth seemed to shake as the giant tree limb hit the pavement.

Caitlin's car came to a stop mere feet from the leafy branches.

Even so, her pulse didn't steady, and she didn't feel any overwhelming relief, for she couldn't pass the obstruction. Throwing a glance over her shoulder, she spotted a flash of lights through the curtain of rain. Instinctively she abandoned the car, leaving its engine running, and began to climb the promontory blindly, not for a moment questioning her direction.

Within seconds she was drenched, her shoes sodden, feet squishing and slipping inside them, yet she plunged on, not bothering to look back. She didn't need to. She could *feel* her pursuer somewhere behind her. All her senses seemed magnified.

So did her fear.

"Bain Morghue, I need your help!"

The words were out of her mouth before she had even thought them. Ridiculous. Crazy. Even if he was still in the area, he wouldn't be able to hear her. And he would more than likely threaten her again, not rescue her.

She could depend on no one but herself.

She could do it. Escape. The dark was her friend, not her enemy. She had to remember that. She was breathing hard, straining from the climb and from the fear that seemed to have become an integral part of her life these past few days. But she was almost over the top. She gave herself a mental push, knew she could lose herself in the castle ruins.

Head down against the wind and rain, she forced herself forward until she thumped into something hard and unyielding, stopping her in her tracks. A human blockade. Familiar.

Bain.

She didn't have to see him. She just knew.

He wrapped an arm around her shoulders and swept her in a half circle. Lightning flashed, revealing his intent face as he mumbled something unintelligible—in another language. Gaelic? More lightning split the sky around them, so bright and blue-white that Caitlin was blinded and hid her face.

She didn't look up when Bain dragged her forward, taking her a few yards away into a space that was protected against the elements. Should she be relieved? Or afraid? If she was to be honest with herself, Caitlin had to admit that she was both.

As Bain continued on through the dark in what seemed to be an underground tunnel, she whispered, "How can you see where you're going without a flashlight?"

"No need for subterfuge," he told her in a normal tone. "You can speak freely. You are safe with me."

As usual, he hadn't given her a direct answer, but this time Caitlin didn't care. Bain knew where he was going, and for the moment, that was good enough for her. Still frightened, she leaned into him until she realized that he was as dry and warm as she was cold and wet. Of course. He'd tucked her under the edge of his cape, which had protected him from the rain. Not wanting to get him as soaked as she was, Caitlin attempted to pull away, but Bain kept her fixed to his side.

"Now is not the time to be prickly."

Despite herself, she started to laugh, in reaction to her mind-numbing fear. He stiffened but kept going. She was still laughing when he stopped and put his hand out. Something clicked, and a door creaked open, revealing a large room lit by flickering light.

Bain let go and Caitlin entered, levity forgotten, eyes widening in awe. At first, she'd thought it the same room as before, but then she recognized what surely must be the great hall of the castle. With a ceiling supported by wooden trusses arched on the bottom and peaked at the top, the room had to be at least thirty feet by seventy—almost as large as a house. It wasn't cold and damp, as one might expect of a stone room on a night like this. Rather, a comforting warmth reached out to her from a wall-sized fireplace big enough for a full-grown person to walk around in.

She automatically moved toward that end, the only area of the room in use. A long, heavy-planked table on one side was covered with candelabra. Rich tapestries, larger and more intricately woven than any she'd seen before, hung from the wall around the fireplace, while a thick woven rug and pillows lay on the floor before it. A mahogany leather couch facing the flames added a modern touch. She rubbed her arms and unsuccessfully tried to keep her teeth from clacking.

"Remove your clothing before you catch your death."

In reaction, Caitlin whipped around, but before she could protest, Bain held out a robe of dark red velvet that he'd produced from somewhere. She took it from him and shivered when their fingers touched.

His eyes were in shadow, but she could feel them touching her, too.

She didn't like the sensation—she was blooming inside like a flower in a hothouse—and yet she felt no distrust for this man who lived in shadows, who couldn't answer even the simplest question in a straightforward manner.

"Turn around," she demanded as she scanned the candlelit room to make certain Ghillie was nowhere in sight.

"You are already in my power, Caitlin," he murmured, his lips turning up in amusement. "You called for me, did you not? You needn't hide from me."

Fear stalked her once more. Fear that he might be right. Fear that he had indeed given her some fairy wine that bound her to him, whether she wanted it or not.

Then he did as she ordered and gave her his back.

Pulling off her soaked jacket, Caitlin quickly replaced her sodden sweater and pants with the robe, wondering what fate had in store for her. Bain hadn't been far from her thoughts since they first met. Perhaps he felt the strong and strange connection, too. Whereas before she had been consumed by fear of physical danger, now some equally dark, disturbing emotion swept through her—fear of her own attraction to him.

"Oh, that feels better," she said, fastening the robe around her damp skin. She kept her tone light. "You can turn around now."

"As I could have any time I pleased." Bain's gaze swept from her to the wet clothing she was holding. He took the dripping garments from her. "They will dry quickly near the fire. As will you." He indicated the pile of pillows.

Caitlin took the couch instead. There she removed her shoes and socks and rubbed her feet dry with the hem of the robe while he hung her clothing on pegs next to the fire, then did the same with his cape. Tonight he wore a full-sleeved midnight-blue velvet shirt with his black pants and boots. The rich garment made him even more handsome, if that was possible. When he turned back to her and saw her safely curled up on the couch, he lifted a brow, but said nothing. He merely swept up her sneakers and socks and placed them on the hearth.

"Now, tell me why you called me," he said, settling on the pillows near her.

She felt like demanding to know how he had heard her over the noise of the storm, but she deemed the question useless. He wouldn't answer, anyway.

"Some man followed me all the way from the standing stones near Lochfynton. I think he wanted to force my car off into the sea."

Bain didn't react as she'd expected. His expression remained passive, slightly pensive, and it sent a chill up her spine. Could he have known? But how?

"That does not explain why you sought *my* aid."

"I don't know." Caitlin shifted her position, drawing her knees to her chest protectively and wrapping her arms around them. She stared into his eyes, tonight as dark a blue as the midnight velvet of his shirt. As much as she might have preferred to lie, she couldn't quite manage it. "I hoped you would help me, I guess." Her exposed feet had grown chilled, and she tried arranging the robe to hang over them.

"Let me."

Before she knew what he was about to do, Bain took hold of her ankles and pulled her feet to his chest. As he warmed them for her, his hands were gentle yet provocative. "We are drawn together by a bond," he said. "A darkness that would frighten most people."

He was frightening her right now. Her skin pulsed with an instant eroticism that took her breath away. The tingling sensation spread. Making her thighs quake. And her breasts tighten. She really should stop him immediately. Only she couldn't.

"I don't believe we are bound," she gasped.

"You deny your own experience, the darkness of the mind you told me you fought?"

"There are different kinds of darkness. Even I am afraid sometimes," she admitted.

His hands stilled and cupped her toes, which now glowed with heat. "But you entered it and brought back one you loved. Tell me about this person."

She might not be willing to discuss Neil, but Ty was a different story. "Ty—my brother—was only seven when it happened. One of his friends was accidentally killed in the school playground, shot by another child playing with his father's gun. Ty was standing next to his friend. Was splattered with his blood. The trauma was too much for him. Ty withdrew. Holed up inside himself. He rarely spoke, stopped relating to other kids. Except me—sometimes. I was twelve, too young to accept losing him forever."

"A difficult time for you both."

Caitlin remembered how she had wept over the loss her parents had tried to make her accept, after months had passed and professional counseling had failed to help Ty. "I refused to give him up to the darkness. I truly believed that if he had someone to cling to, someone to come back to, eventually he would. I read him stories and told him tales about spells being broken and obstacles overcome by magic. I spent every free moment I had with him, praying, hoping, believing that magic could break the spell that had stolen Ty from our family."

"And you succeeded."

"Eventually. Though Ty has never forgotten what happened. It still affects him. He's quiet, and keeps to himself a lot, but he's not lost, like he once was. In my heart, I can't help believing magic brought him back to us."

"There is wondrous magic to be found in this world if you believe. Not many would have been so brave. 'Twas you who were the magic for your brother," he said softly.

Hands on her ankles once more, Bain tugged, sliding Caitlin off the couch and onto his lap. Her heart pounded more wildly than it had during the drive over the sea loch road. Surely he could hear its beating. His hand smoothed her still-damp hair from her face. He cupped her cheek. Drank from her eyes. Her gaze was locked with his. She looked deep, deep inside, past the midnight blue, to their dark centers. She read desire there, desire and something more. Something dark and inexplicable.

He masked her view into his soul by crushing his mouth over hers. Their tongues danced to a rhythm older than time. Her arms wound around his neck as though they belonged there. A faint voice asked what she thought she was doing, giving herself over to a stranger, a mysterious midnight rider whom no one knew. He could do anything to her. Anything. And who would be the wiser?

And why didn't she care?

All she cared for was the taste of his mouth, the feel of his flesh against her fingers, the beat of his heart as it sang with hers. When his hand slipped down from her cheek to her neck and then to the opening of her robe, she adjusted her body to allow him to stroke her tender flesh. To find her lace-encased breast, her aching nipple. His fingers left a trail of fire where they touched her sensitive skin.

Fairy fire.

He slid a hand up the inside of her thighs, and instinctively she parted them, allowing him access. He made a sound deep in his throat...then suddenly raised his head.

And she was amazed when, with obvious effort, he pushed her away.

"That should not have happened," Bain muttered. "We should not be so intimate, when we canna be together."

"Why not?" she asked, before realizing the implications of her question.

He set her from him, rose, then helped her to her feet. "Your clothing should be dry. You can dress, and I will take you to your vehicle."

"Why don't you ever answer a person's questions?" Angry at him for making her want more—and at herself for not resisting—Caitlin spun toward the fireplace and retrieved her clothes. "It really ticks me, the way you play all mysterious when it suits you. Are you trying to hide something? What's your problem? Will you please answer me for once?"

Bain turned to her, his expression bleak. "I, lady, am lost in a darkness from which there is no escape."

CHAPTER FOUR

The words were out of his mouth before he could stop them. Bain followed the admission with an old Gaelic curse as he stared into great green eyes that had gone all wide and soft on him. Plumbing their depths, he read a compassion there that found uncomfortable rest within his being.

"No escape?" Caitlin murmured, her intent to change out of the robe seemingly forgotten for the moment. She dropped the garments onto the couch. "From what?"

Her robe slipped a bit on her shoulder, revealing soft white flesh. He took a deep breath, knowing he should be heeding the heat in his groin, not testing the honesty of a stranger. What a foolish impulse. The story of the brother and the lady's heroism had obviously affected him more deeply than he cared to acknowledge. He hadn't known such a love was possible. He was used to dealing with those who put self-interest and greed above everything else.

"'Twas only a figure of speech."

"Is *this* your darkness?" She glanced about, as if really seeing her surroundings for the first time. "This crumbling castle? Or is it something more?"

His heart beat swiftly at her insight. Not that he would confirm any conjecture she might make. "Sometimes we are trapped by circumstances."

"Circumstances," she echoed, "or our own actions?"

Her gaze narrowed, and he sensed that she mentally took a step backward in an effort to break their fragile connection.

"Some crime, perhaps? Is that what you meant?"

"You have quite an imagination."

"We already established that, but I'm not drawing on my ingenuity now," she told him. "Rumor is there's an escaped convict hanging around the area. One who's dangerous and desperate. I was warned he might be using Black Broch as his cover."

Though he wouldn't give her the truth at any rate, Bain knew a moment's disappointment. "So you think me a criminal. Do I look desperate, lady?" Purposely he turned his most intimidating expression on her. He was not surprised in the least when she held her ground, only the fluttering of her lashes and the deepening of her breath indicating that he had any effect on her at all. "Do I frighten you?"

That she lifted her chin and said, "Evasive, as usual, but then what did I expect?" amused him.

For now it was she who was avoiding giving direct answers.

Bain had no doubt that he did frighten this Caitlin Montgomery, no matter how brave a face she showed him. He observed it through her eyes...a fear that went far deeper than mere concern for her skin. Lovely, soft skin, he thought, distracted for a moment by his urge to sample it yet again. This fright went all the way to her very soul, and he guessed he was not the original source, but rather the immediate catalyst. She had reason to distrust. Another man?

Bain hated the thought.

Hated that he could care.

He'd gone too long without a woman. None had ever gotten past his natural armor before. This one was making him feel things best left alone...and far too easily for his peace of mind.

"You remind me of a bully I once knew," Caitlin said. "He wanted people to be afraid of him so they couldn't see through him...couldn't guess that he was nearly consumed by his own demons."

Another start, again covered by a laugh. "And what would you have me fear?"

She shook her head, and the drying strands of her hair snaked around her shoulders. "I don't know. Yet."

"I am certain you shall herald the truth from the very walls of Black Broch, should you think you've discovered it."

She didn't answer, and Bain grew uneasy. Fears. Yes, he had his share.

And, even linked to him as casually as she was, Caitlin had every reason to be afraid. Throughout his lifetime, many had sought and plotted to give themselves the opportunity to claim his ancestral legacy. But none was so powerful as the one who challenged him presently. They'd met before. Several times. And with each foray, his enemy grew more determined.

And, Bain worried, stronger.

His enemy would make mincemeat of a lovely young lass like Caitlin, should she stand in his way.

Bain knew that banishing Caitlin from Black Broch for her own sake would be the wisest course. But he couldn't. 'Twas more than the emerald green of her eyes and the flame of her red hair and her sleek and silky limbs that made him want to take her, to make her his forever.

Her fiery spirit... her heartfelt loyalty... her ability to love selflessly...

These were the qualities that made him long for the life Caitlin could show him, a life he could not, as things stood, have. These were the things that inspired guilt, a new experience for him. For these were also the things that made him hold on to her a bit longer, even if he kept himself from taking her in every sense of the word. For, the almighty powers help him, they would then both be lost.

"Get dressed," he said, abruptly striding away from her. "I shall return momentarily."

Though she thought to, Caitlin didn't object. Instead, she silently watched Bain retreat, his back straight, his head held high, his stride long. First he'd dismissed her, and now he didn't give her so much as a glance before leaving the room through a far door she hadn't noticed earlier.

All this talk of fear made it seem less real. Made him seem more human. She paused at that. What an odd thought. Human. As if he weren't.

Why had he terminated their conversation so abruptly? Had she struck too close to home? Was he like the bully she'd mentioned, all bravado to hide his own frailties? Maybe. But there was more to him. She wouldn't make the mistake of underestimating Bain Morghue. Not as she had Neil. She tried never to make the same mistake twice.

Quickly she changed back into her sweater and pants, then pulled her fingertips through her almost dry hair to fluff it out. If only she had a mirror and a comb. And lipstick wouldn't be out of order, either.

But as he swept back into the room, Bain gave her the feeling that she looked just fine. More than fine. His deep blue eyes glinted appreciatively as they swept over her, coming to rest on her face as he stopped before her.

Whatever she'd been expecting, it hadn't been for him to demand, "Give me your right hand."

"What?"

"Are you deaf, lass? Your hand."

When she didn't comply, he reached for it. His fingers were warm and strong—though unthreatening—when he tugged at her wrist. His mere touch fired her blood, and she was certain he knew it. Not that he indicated any such thing. No twinkle in his eyes. No blatant quiver to his lips. His expression might be stone, but he knew. She was certain.

Feeling something slide over her middle finger, she tore her gaze free and looked down.

"Oh." She glanced at his face, which was still impassive, then back at the heavy metal ring, which immediately warmed to her skin. "It's...wonderful."

A graceful silver falcon turned in a flurry of feathers, clutching a milky white moonstone in its talons. She lifted her hand toward the firelight, and a subtle blue immediately winked from its depths. The detailing of the falcon itself—multiple layers of feathers, resembling the intertwining spirals of ancient Celtic design—was superb.

"I wish I had designed this." She stared at Bain in wonder that he had such an object, the kind of thing she herself would love to create. "Who is the artist?"

"Someone no longer of this world."

Dead? "Pity." Although carefully polished, the ring did look very old. "I would give anything to see more of this person's work."

"Perhaps you shall have that opportunity."

Mesmerized by the hint of promise in his tone—did he own such like pieces, then?—she met his gaze and caught her breath. Raw desire stared back at her, drawing a curl of warmth from her belly and a damp flush between her thighs. Embarrassed, Caitlin looked away, concentrated on the ring and started to slip it from her finger.

"No." He caught her hand and shoved the silver over her knuckle again. "'Tis yours."

"I couldn't—"

"You must. And you mustn't remove it, not even while you sleep."

"Not take it off?" He was still holding on to her, making it nearly impossible for her to think. "Why not?"

"You said you believe in magic, Caitlin Montgomery. Were you truthful with me?"

Breathless, she slipped her hand free. "I'm to believe this is a magical ring? What's it supposed to do? Drive off other falcons?"

"In a manner of speaking."

"Strange, but I would've bet you didn't have a whimsical bone in your body."

He frowned her quivery grin away. "Don't make light, lady. I gave you this token to keep you safe. While you wear it, I can protect you."

"So are you the falcon? Or the hunter?"

She'd meant it as a joke, to loosen him up, but he didn't appear amused. His expression was dead serious. A strange foreboding flitted through her, and she felt compelled to do as he demanded.

Even so, she tried to argue. "It's a little heavy."

Like magic, the ring's weight lightened until she could barely tell it wrapped around her finger... as if it had subtly become part of her.

"My enemies will not dare touch you as long as you wear my token. Take it off, and..."

That he didn't finish the sentence chilled her. She remembered thinking earlier that his enemies were her enemies. Someone had lain in wait for her barely an hour before. Someone had tried to force her into the loch.

Someone *he* knew?

His enemy?

"You're a dangerous man to be around in more ways than one, aren't you?"

"Best that you not forget so."

Before she could question him further, he picked up her coat and slipped it about her shoulders, his fingers lingering a little too long, his breath warm on the back of her neck. She shivered. But then, as if he were having second thoughts about any hesitation, he swept her from the room. A moment later, the darkness cloaked them both. Even when they exited the tunnel into the still, dry night, Bain held her fast. That he was dangerous, Caitlin did not doubt. And yet she had no desire to shrug free of him. She felt oddly connected to him, as if they were one somehow. The thought was both scary and exhilarating.

"So where's your faithful steed?" she asked breathlessly, searching the area for the big black stallion.

"I believe you have your own steed—uh, auto."

"Stopped dead by a tree. Lightning struck a major limb, and the resulting mess blocked the road. I was forced to abandon my car."

Caitlin tried not to worry that the man who'd been chasing her might now be lying in wait. She had the Morghue for protection, after all, and she knew how fierce he could be when his anger was aroused.

"It'll take several men or even mechanical equipment to clear the way again," she speculated.

"We shall see."

They traversed the uneven ground in silence for the several minutes it took to crest the final hill, where she finally caught sight of her car. The engine was still running and the lights were still on, illuminating several leafy branches. To Caitlin's confusion, the tree limb looked to be far smaller than she remembered. Its branches didn't come close to blocking the entire width of the road.

"Talk about imagination," she muttered, taking the lead on the way downhill. "I could have gotten around this mess if only I had tried."

"Fear intensifies emotions and perceptions."

Caitlin thought perhaps the limb would appear larger from the vantage point of the car. But the angle made no difference. It seemed her perception had been off about tenfold.

"At least the creep didn't take my keys, and I haven't run out of gas," she muttered, checking things out.

She picked up her sketchbook from where it had slid onto the floor, glancing through the windshield as she set it on the passenger seat.

Before her, Bain grabbed hold of the limb and, seemingly without real difficulty, inched it away from the car. Not wanting to appear weak and docile, Caitlin immediately jumped to help. While awkward, the task wasn't nearly as difficult as she had imagined it would be.

A moment later, they stood by her vehicle, and she had no more excuses to delay her departure. She stared up at Bain, at his moon-silvered profile, and something within her mourned his imminent loss.

"When shall I see you again?" Caitlin asked. Not *if* but *when*, for she couldn't imagine not seeing him.

"Whenever you wish."

"What? I rub this ring and you appear like some kind of a genie?"

"Genie?"

What she could see of his expression, by the moonlight peering from between a moving sky of clouds, was genuinely puzzled. So he wasn't up on his fairy tales.

"Never mind. Maybe I'll just put my two lips together and blow," she teased, remembering Lauren Bacall's old line.

"I am no dog, lady, but a man."

His expression had turned indignant. He wasn't a movie buff, either.

"I'll figure something out," she muttered, wondering if he was truly humorless.

She started to get into the car, only to have him suddenly grab her and mold her against his length. A kiss? She raised her lips expectantly, her heart pounding.

But then, just as suddenly, he let her go with a growl. "I will know when you need me." He strode off into the darkness.

She turned in a circle, seeking him. But he had well and truly disappeared. Vanished, as smoothly and silently as he had come to her rescue when she needed him.

I will know when you need me.

The words echoed through her mind. Almost as if she had imagined them . . . if not the entire episode.

But no, the storm had struck the tree limb that now rested at its base. The evidence sat there, before her eyes. Remembering that someone had instigated this latest encounter with Bain, someone who'd been after her and might still be lurking nearby, she quickly slid into the driver's seat and locked the doors. As she did so, her gaze met the ring. Bain's ring. More proof.

Caitlin started the car and turned it toward the B and B.

Why was she always giving herself a hard time when it came to Bain Morghue? Why did she question his very existence, as if he weren't really part of this world?

The questions plagued her as she drove. She was becoming obsessed with this man, who stood apart from any other she'd known. And yet the situations she'd been finding herself in lately felt all too familiar, and too close for comfort. But she didn't want to think she was repeating the mistake. She didn't want to believe the psychologist who had told her she was attracted to troubled men as a result of her intense relationship with her brother. This time was different, she assured herself.

Strange how far a good dose of adrenaline could go toward addling one's brain. Almost as effective as fairy wine ... or Bain's home brew.

Home at last.

The cottage loomed before her, a pale blue-white. Caitlin stopped the rental car near the front door. Cutting the engine, she shot a penetrating look around the nearby grounds, wishing she could see into every cranny and shadow. She felt safe enough, though she might very well be fooling herself into thinking she had nothing to worry about.

For even if Bain's ring could protect her from his so-called enemies, who would protect her from him?

"What an unusual design!" Mary exclaimed when she noticed the ring during breakfast the next morning. "Might I be having a closer look?"

Uncomfortable with the attention Bain's talisman brought, Caitlin set down the basket of scones and reluctantly gave the hostess her hand. Mary gingerly touched a fingertip to the intricately fashioned falcon.

"Ah, such fine work. Why didn't you ever show this to us before?"

"It's not mine," Caitlin said without thinking. "Er...I didn't design it. One of your countrymen did."

She assumed one had, though Bain hadn't gone into details. Now, as Alistair and Julian and the Abernathys took turns admiring the ring from a distance, she hoped no one would question her more closely.

That hope went unanswered when Alistair asked, "You acquired this yesterday?" His gaze was pinned to the piece, as if it troubled him.

"I couldn't resist." She hoped he wouldn't ask where she'd gotten it. She didn't want to lie outright.

When he looked up at her, his brow was furrowed and his dark brown eyes held a strange glint. "I'm surprised you found the time, what with all the activities you had planned."

"Now, Alistair," Mary said, "'tis always possible for a clever lass to squeeze in a wee bit of time for shopping."

With a grunt of acknowledgment, her husband settled back in his chair. But Caitlin couldn't help but wonder at his thoughts. For some reason, the ring seemed to disturb him.

"Would you allow me a closer look?" Julian asked, quickly grasping her hand when she again reached for the scone basket. "Hmm...it appears to be an old piece that might be very valuable indeed."

Though she had no doubt but that it was old, Caitlin returned, "Or a good, newer copy," and reclaimed her hand.

"Then the seller didn't say?" When she shrugged noncommittally, Julian reminded her, "I deal in antiques. If you would take it off for a moment..."

Caitlin almost did as the Englishman suggested to finish the matter, but then she remembered Bain's admonition not to remove the ring. Foolish, for who among this household could be his enemy? No one here had even heard of him. Even so, she couldn't bring herself to defy him in this matter.

"Actually, I really don't care if it's an antique or not," she murmured.

"But you might have been cheated."

"Then I would rather not know," she said. "Whatever its history, I am satisfied with the ring."

But Julian didn't look any more satisfied than Alistair had. She glanced across the table at the Abernathys. The professor was concentrating on buttering a scone, as if he hadn't heard a word of the discussion...or was purposely ignoring the quietly building tension at the table. His wife merely looked as nervous as Caitlin was beginning to feel.

What was the big deal here?

The door to the kitchen swung open to allow Bridget passage. She was carrying a platter filled with eggs and sausages. On reflex, Caitlin slid her right hand into her lap before the servant could spot it and make another of her dire pronouncements.

Good heavens, now *she* was being paranoid!

Maybe so, but she was thankful when Bridget left the room and Mary tactfully turned the topic to everyone's plans for the day. Caitlin let the others take center stage, and only when pressed said she was too tired to play tourist and would stick close by to sketch.

"Wherever you go, please be careful," Mary warned them all. "Especially you ladies with your handbags."

"Oh, my..." Mrs. Abernathy blanched. "Is there a pickpocket around?"

"City crazies," Alistair growled. "From Glasgow, and even Edinburgh. They come through every once in a while to have themselves a little fun at our expense. They bother the livestock, if not the people."

"Skinheads," Julian muttered, frowning.

"Fiona MacGregor said a couple of the hooligans were in her shop yesterday." Mary clucked and tucked a stray strand of brown hair back into its knot. "Then a tourist complained to the officials that her handbag had been stolen by one of them. He cut the straps right off her arm!"

Coming from a big city herself, Caitlin wasn't particularly worried, though she promised to keep an eye out for the "crazies."

But for the entire morning she was as good as her word and didn't leave sight of the MacDonalds' place. She spread a blanket on a hillock and sketched her surroundings to her heart's content. The manor. The cottages. The formal arrangements of azaleas, rhododendrons, fuchsias and camellias in a nearby walled garden.

Rather than making sketches for her designs, she was creating memories for herself.

Memories—she would have many to take home with her, but she suspected the most vivid would be of Bain Morghue. She stared down at the ring he had given her to keep her safe. He wanted to protect her, not to hurt her.

Not like Neil.

Though she'd come to Scotland in part to get over what had happened, she couldn't keep from thinking about that disastrous relationship.

Attending family therapy with her parents and brother a few times the year before, she'd met another patient in the waiting room. Neil Howard had been handsome and intelligent, if darkly intense. That very intensity had intrigued her, and she'd agreed to see him.

The closer they drew together, the more demanding, jealous and aggressive Neil became. Caitlin tried her best to understand, thinking he would come around and truly trust her, given time and more therapy. Neil told her he was seeing the psychologist to get over his mistrust because of another woman's betrayal. But, unready to tell her everything yet, he gave few details.

The crisis came when Neil claimed that someone was after him, that he needed to leave town to hide out and Caitlin had to come with him. When she told him she had no intention of leaving her home, and encouraged him to seek help from the authorities, he turned on her. Either she was with him or against him.

And if she refused to come with him, he would kill her.

Luckily, a neighbor heard them arguing and called the police. But Caitlin never knew what part of Neil's story was the truth and what was fabrication, because he was killed shortly after making bail. She'd never found out who shot him or why.

Guilt-ridden, she discussed the problem in a private session with Ty's psychologist, Dr. Hoffman, who suggested Caitlin might be attracted to troubled men—that perhaps she'd been so traumatized by her brother's withdrawal and her involvement in his recovery that she looked for similar, familiar relationships.

Caitlin readily admitted she had never considered giving up on Neil, any more than she had on Ty. And yet Neil had actually been killed. That meant he'd been *in* trouble, not merely troubled.

Dr. Hoffman insisted that Neil had been delusional and suggested he might have been too aggressive with the wrong person, thereby ensuring his own death or perhaps he'd been using drugs.... Whatever the truth, Caitlin realized she had a problem she needed to deal with, in that she hadn't listened to her own intuition about Neil in the first place.

That was why her attraction to Bain troubled her so. He was more intense and secretive and dangerous than Neil had ever seemed. And yet she could not deny her growing fascination with the man.

Was the fact that Bain Morghue reminded her of Neil Howard mere coincidence? Or had she subconsciously sought a man like him, to repeat her mistake? Or to prove she could do things differently, given another chance?

When she looked down at her pad, Caitlin was startled. While thinking about Bain, she had subconsciously drawn him as she had first seen him. Fog swirling around him, he was seated on his stallion. She'd caught every plane of his face, every nuance of his mesmerizing expression, perfectly. His billowing cape gave him an air of power and daring and mystery. Here was a man to catch any woman's fancy.

Suddenly, a fabulous idea came to her.

Abstracting bits and pieces of the sketch separately—the horse's head, Bain's profile in silhouette, the hilt of his fantastic sword—she could combine them with traditional twining Celtic designs like leaves and spirals and sacred circles and work them into a fabulous demon-lover theme. The idea would work especially well for larger pieces of jewelry, such as brooches and pendants and belt buckles, as well as for purses and scarves.

Caitlin grinned. She could imagine Bain's reaction if she told him he was the inspiration for a new line of jewelry and accessories based on an old legend! He would probably threaten her with dire consequences.

Her growling stomach signaled her hunger, and she took that as a sign that she should leave both her uneasy speculations and her creative ideas for a while and drive into Droon for lunch. Gathering up her blanket, she slung it over her shoulder and made her way toward the cottage. Halfway there, she spotted Alistair leaving the manor and heading for his car.

He saw her, too. With a wave, he called, "Caitlin, have you time for a word?"

"Sure." Caitlin veered off in that direction.

Alistair waited for her, his lips flattened into a straight line beneath his mustache. "About your new ring," he said, his voice gruff. "I thought it looked familiar when you showed it to us this morning."

Worried that he would say it had been stolen, or something of the sort, Caitlin immediately grew uneasy. "Really?"

"Aye. You know how local history and legends interest me. My library is full of reference books and magazines and articles on the subject. I went through some of my materials, and sure enough, I found it.''

"A picture of the ring?"

His shook his grizzled head. "The photo was of a sketch of the falcon.''

Relieved, Caitlin grew more enthusiastic, despite Alistair's continuing dour expression. "What's so special about it?''

"Well, now. A while back, a comely young woman named Janet Drummond lived nearby with her husband, who was neither so young nor so comely himself. As the story goes, Janet liked to sketch to please herself. No one was much impressed with her work, least of all her husband, who thought she should be putting her time to better use.''

"Quite a few people have that opinion about artists,'' Caitlin said. "Sorry. Go on.''

"Well, now, Janet started disappearing, sometimes for a day, sometimes for a week or more. And when she would return, she had new sketches for her collection. They grew quite fanciful, and were very good, as well, especially those of a mysterious, caped man on a great dark horse.''

A caped man on a horse? Having just sketched Bain like that, she caught her breath.

Alistair concluded, "The falcon was the last sketch she made before disappearing altogether.''

A chill crept through Caitlin. She couldn't shake the feeling of dread the statement brought. Bain had said the ring's designer was no longer of this world. "So someone started using her sketches for jewelry designs?''

"Nae.'' Alistair frowned, and his dark eyes nearly pierced her with their intensity. "I couldn't find such a reference, at any rate. Most of the sketches disappeared with Janet, except for the few she'd given to friends. And the falcon. She left that one on the front door, as if to guard the cottage until she returned. Only she never did. Some say she ran off with a handsome young lover—the mysterious man in her drawings—for good.''

Wondering if Alistair had found sketches of the mystery man, as well, Caitlin asked, ''When did this happen?''

''Nearly a century ago.''

Too long ago for it to be Bain. She took a relieved breath. ''Quite a story.'' And one she wondered if Bain knew.

''Aye. 'Twas said that those times Janet disappeared, she walked the paths of Black Broch.'' Alistair's expression was dark. ''I canna help but wish a pretty young thing like you wouldn't wander about the place alone.''

Caitlin didn't think it sounded like a request. She forced a smile to her lips. ''I thought you weren't superstitious.''

'''Tis a bad feeling I'm having about the Broch lately, is all. And now your having the ring made from Janet Drummond's drawing is right peculiar. Bridget would call it a sign, for certain.''

Thinking Alistair sounded every bit as superstitious as the maid, if only more restrained about it, Caitlin said, ''I'll keep your advice in mind.'' She was making no promises.

''You do that. A pretty lass wandering alone isn't safe anyplace these days. But Black Broch . . . your going there is asking for trouble.'' Alistair opened the car door. "I'll be going to town to pick up some supplies. Anything I can get you?"

Not liking his tone, Caitlin said coolly, "Actually, I was going that way myself for lunch."

"I can offer you a ride."

"Thanks, but I wouldn't want to hold you up." And, speaking of being alone, Caitlin didn't particularly want to be alone with Alistair. The conversation, and his warning, made her uneasy. "I'm not sure what else I might decide to do after I eat."

Like wandering around Black Broch. Alone. Despite Alistair's warning and her own reservations because of Neil, Caitlin knew she couldn't stay away from the place—or from Bain—for long.

CHAPTER FIVE

But Bain was nowhere to be found.

After lunch, Caitlin left her car at the bed-and-breakfast and set off for the crossroads on foot. Exercise was all she got for her trouble. The ruins of Black Broch stood empty. And, if the truth be known, Caitlin didn't have any desire to stick around and wait for Bain to show.

Alistair had her well and truly spooked.

Refusing to let him ruin her afternoon, however, she walked another mile or so through a pretty little glen. She made herself comfortable near a stream crossing the middle of a sheep pasture, where she continued working on her demon-lover theme. Engrossed in playing with the possible combinations, never quite satisfied with her designs, she didn't realize how late it had grown until the light began to fade. Only when she felt herself straining to see did she realize that the sun had set and the air had developed a distinctive chill.

Securing her sketchbook under her arm, she set off for home, but she hadn't gotten far before raucous barking and frightened bleating drew her attention. She left the footpath and slid through a crude wooden fence to enter another rolling pasture. Climbing to the top of a small knoll, she saw them—three of Alistair's "city crazies" setting a large dog of indeterminate breed on some sheep that were clearly confused and running scared.

The men were young, in their late teens or early twenties, she guessed. Two sported heads barely stubbled with hair. One was bare-chested but for a vest, while the second wore a leather jacket hung with several chains. The third had his hair cut into a Mohawk, and dyed a brilliant yellow and orange that practically glowed in contrast with his black T-shirt. Looking across the field past them, Caitlin spotted their old junker of a car on the gravel road.

The Mohawked thug shouted and gave the dog a hand signal. The animal set after a ewe and her lamb.

Planning to hurry back to the MacDonalds', where she would call the local constable, Caitlin froze when a shaggy old man with long, matted gray hair crested the hill opposite.

Shaking his staff at the young troublemakers, he yelled, "Away from my flock! Away, I say!"

Derisive laughter carried straight to her, and as if by silent consensus, the three began stalking the shepherd. The guy with the Mohawk whistled for the dog, who immediately forgot his current prey and ran to his master, the obvious leader of the group. Now Caitlin was torn. She didn't really want to get involved with such tough-looking characters, and yet how could she justify leaving a defenseless old man alone in the face of such a threat?

She found herself jogging straight for trouble even as the shepherd was surrounded. "Hey, there, what's going on?" she called out, as if she hadn't a clue.

The one in the leather jacket spun around to challenge her. "Who be wantin' ta know?"

Realizing that to show any sign of uncertainty would be unwise, Caitlin demanded, "Who are *you?*" Brash words to drown out the loud thumping of her heart.

"Hey, an American!" the tough one in the vest said.

"Go away, lass," cried the shepherd, "before they hurt ye!"

She stopped, but didn't retreat.

"Nae, we wouldn't hurt a lovely lassie, now would we, boyos?" Mohawk signaled to his companions to alter their direction.

Now they were intent on cornering *her*.

Though her instincts told her to back off, Caitlin stood her ground, hoping to shame them. "Some tough guys you are, hassling helpless sheep, an old man and a woman."

"Easy pickin's," the guy in the leather jacket agreed. "We don't like ta work too hard."

Her stomach knotted, and a queasy feeling spread through her fast. What now? She'd rushed into the situation without planning a strategy.

"Why don't you boys go back where you belong before you get into trouble?" she suggested, without any real hope that they would.

Mohawk grinned. "And miss out on a wee bit o' fun? Nae, I don't rightly think so."

Maybe she could outrun them. But as she stared at the spiked dog collar he wore around his neck, she found it difficult even to breathe. "I've called the constable!" she lied, looking for an escape.

"Not bloody likely," the one in the vest spit out.

Caitlin noted that he had several safety pins threaded through his right ear, and swastikas tattooed on each forearm. They really did look like skinheads!

What had she gotten herself into?

"Leave the lass be!" the shepherd shouted, now following the toughs with his staff raised in *her* defense.

The guy in the leather jacket turned, grabbed the rod and shoved the old man hard, causing him to fall to his knees, groaning.

Caitlin edged away, looking for a way out so that she could go get help, but she'd waited too long. Giving the dog a hand signal that sent him flying behind to cut off her escape, Mohawk lunged at her. She slipped from his determined grasp, only to trip on the uneven ground and lose her balance. Her sketchpad flew from her hand to land flipped open several feet away.

Though she tried, Caitlin couldn't catch herself. A spill to the rocky ground made her cry out when her hip came into contact with something hard and sharp. As the gang closed in on her, she looked around for anything she could use as a makeshift weapon.

"Don't come near me!" she said, brandishing a rock and scooting backward.

The leader's narrow gaze focused on her hand. "Hey, boyos, take a look at the lassie's fancy ring."

The one in the leather jacket whistled. "Must be worth more'n a quid or two."

Mohawk held out an imperious hand to Caitlin. "Come, now, give it over."

Thinking she had to be crazy to refuse, Caitlin shook her head and brandished the rock more fiercely. The moonstone in her ring glowed a brilliant blue against the gray dusk.

Mohawk slid something from his pocket. There was a sharp click and then she saw it—a nasty-looking stiletto blade.

Her mouth went dry.

Wielding the knife her way, he snarled threateningly, "I'll cut it off if'n you like."

Wildly looking around for escape, Caitlin's eyes alit on the sketch she'd drawn of the midnight horseman slicing through the fog.

So where was Bain Morghue when she needed him?

The rhythmic beat of horse's hooves behind her was her answer. A disbelieving Caitlin whipped around to see Bain crest the knoll. His features set in a mask of fury, he reined in his horse to survey the situation. The great beast whinnied in protest and pranced in place, his muscles gathering to lift his forequarters. When he reared, his front hooves flashed as menacingly as his master's eyes.

"So, boyos, you have a fondness for pretty blades, do you?" Bain thundered. In a flash, he lifted his vicious-looking claymore.

"Yiii!" Mouth and eyes almost comically wide, Mohawk dropped the stiletto and ran for his life.

The others raced him for the safety of the car.

Uttering a war whoop that resounded through the glen, Bain charged forward, brandishing his weapon over his head. He led the horse through their midst, made a pass at the leader and brushed him so hard, he fell. Then he did the same to the other two. They had difficulty rising—the one in the vest slunk along the ground like the vermin he was—and Caitlin imagined they were screaming as loudly as their bully of a dog by the time they scrambled into their beat-up vehicle.

She joined the shepherd, who was likewise on his feet now, and watched the car drive off. "Are you all right?" she asked the man.

"Thanks to ye and the laird, aye."

Startled that he knew Bain's identity, Caitlin thought to question the old man, but before she could do so, the horse thundered toward them, stopping mere inches away from them. Bain was looking at both of them with concern.

"Those hooligans woulda made ground sausage of me if the lass hadna stopped 'em," the shepherd told Bain. "She coulda run, but she helped me instead. She's a bonny brave lass."

Bain turned a thoughtful eye on Caitlin. "Aye, that she is, Auld Sandy."

Auld Sandy? The crazy old shepherd the chemist had told her about.

"And I'll be thanking ye both for my lovelies, as well," he said, retrieving his staff. "Kate and Maeve and Linette and Betty and Alanna and the rest."

Caitlin realized he was speaking of his flock. If the situation hadn't been so grave, she might have smiled.

Dismounting, Bain said, "You take care of your lassies, now."

"Aye, that I will, Laird Morghue."

Old Sandy retreated, making a *baaa*ing sound. The ewes and lambs quickly fell in behind him, forming a small procession toward the nearest knoll. And Caitlin remembered the chemist telling her that the shepherd's ewes followed him out of love. All were quickly swallowed up by the growing dark.

Turning, she realized Bain was staring at her intently. A flush making her cheeks burn with warmth, she looked down at her hands and realized the ring's moonstone no longer glowed blue. Its milky white reflected the pale moon above.

How odd.

Frowning, she said, "It seems that Auld Sandy knows you, even if the other villagers don't." Even if he was purportedly a crazy old man.

"We've met before." And before she could ask him when and under what circumstances, he turned the tables on her. "But being that he's a stranger to you, why did you put yourself in such danger?"

Since he was making to dismount, Bain's back was to her, and she couldn't tell whether or not he disapproved.

"Auld Sandy was in trouble," Caitlin said, retrieving her sketchbook from where it had flown. "I acted on instinct, as any decent human being would. What about you? Why did you come to the rescue?"

Lightly touching ground, he turned to her. "You needed me," he said simply.

And she realized the avowal pleased her. "But I'm practically a stranger to you."

"Nae, lady, 'tis as if you're a part of me."

His moon-silvered expression was serious. And somewhat perplexed. Never having seen him appear the least bit uncertain before, Caitlin didn't know how to respond. At the moment, she sensed Bain was open, emotionally unguarded.

Because of her.

A thrill shot through her. She had the power to affect this man who could be a strong and fierce adversary. He was also very territorial.

'Tis as if you're a part of me.

Or did he think she *belonged* to him?

Her heart was beating wildly again—out of a fear more potent than that inspired by any skinheads. A fear that was also a deep longing. A knowledge that part of her wouldn't mind belonging to him.

"I can't," she whispered. "Won't."

"Won't?" he echoed, frowning. "Won't what?"

Wouldn't give up the control that had always been hers. For Caitlin knew that if she were further involved with this man, she could too easily become his for good.

"Be late." Her lie was a whisper against the night. "I must get back...."

"I shall escort you to your lodgings."

"No, that's not necessary." Any longer in his company, and she might lose what was left of her good sense. "I got out here on my own, and—"

"You should choose your arguments wisely, lady." His expression was grave. "You cannot win them all. You could lose yourself in the dark, and I would be obligated to come to your rescue yet again this night."

So he was determined. She heard no room for negotiation in his tone. Irritated, she muttered, "Fine," and took off.

Just as quickly, he caught her arm, grinding her to a halt. "'Twould be faster to ride." He called to the horse in the foreign tongue Caitlin had heard him speak before.

"No!" she protested. She couldn't trust herself so close to Bain again. She remembered the night they'd met. The enchanted ride. The magical kiss afterward. Too dangerous. "I need the exercise to get rid of all that extra adrenaline."

"Then I shall walk with you."

He let her go and allowed her to set the pace. Then he fell in step with her. His mount followed several yards behind, softly blowing through his nose, as if content.

"What's your horse's name?"

"In English ... Raven."

"So you *were* speaking Gaelic?" When he nodded, she went on to a far more important question. "I was thinking of you just seconds before you appeared. Odd, isn't it? Almost as if you could read my mind."

"The mind can be a strong tool when used to its fullest capacity."

"But you came so quickly."

"I was in the area."

"Strange. I didn't hear your horse's hoofbeats until the very moment I needed you."

"You were preoccupied."

"And the ring. It was glowing blue." As if it were sending a signal, she thought.

"Reflecting your heightened emotions."

"Like a mood ring?" When he furrowed his brow as if he didn't understand, she reminded him, "Very popular in the early seventies. Only I never heard of a *moonstone* turning colors like that."

"Not all moonstones are magic."

She couldn't tell whether or not he was teasing her. "What do you know of magic?"

He laughed softly. The sound held a touch of irony. "You would be surprised, lass."

"Try me."

"Why, the very land around us is enchanted, don't ye know?" His voice was mesmerizing, taking on more of a burr than usual. "'Tis said islands off the coast sometimes disappear, and then, years or decades or even centuries later, they reappear."

Who hadn't heard such legends? But she wanted his opinion. "So where do they supposedly go when they disappear?"

"Nowhere. They become part of the invisible world."

"A world that mortals cannot see, of course."

"Unless they be particularly wise or pure of heart."

Grinning at his seriousness, she chose to play along. "How...enchanting. So you're saying Scotland is some kind of a fairy land?"

"Only certain areas—sacred groves, ancient hills, deep, dark springs—anywhere the fey dominates the real."

"And have you seen this so-called invisible world yourself?" She strained her eyes to gauge his reaction through the dark.

But instead of giving her a direct answer, he said, "You are not a woman who believes in only those things you can see, brave Caitlin, or you would not have been able to save your brother. You would not have even tried."

A compliment? Or an attempt to distract her? "I'm not the subject here," she reminded him as they approached the main road back to the B and B. "Why don't you like talking about yourself?"

"There are many things that interest me more."

"What about your family, then?" She was determined to get something concrete about his life out of him. Other people could see him—she had witnessed it—but she wanted even more solidity. "Do you have any siblings?"

"Not of full blood."

"So your parents divorced and remarried?"

"My father died."

"I'm sorry."

"No need. 'Twas a long time ago. I barely remember him."

"But your mother is still alive?" she prodded as they turned onto the asphalt road toward home.

"Aye."

"Do you realize that's three personal questions in a row you've actually answered," she said wonderingly. "You surprise me."

"Sometimes, lady, I surprise myself."

Bain realized he'd done something he hadn't meant to—had opened up a wee bit more than was wise to this woman who captivated him. That wouldn't do. Not at all. There was safety in a certain amount of ignorance, he thought, reminded of that fact when they reached the crossroads and he glanced up at Black Broch.

Safety for both of them.

So when she urged, "Tell me about your mother," he thought to change the subject. Then again, more avoidance would only make her more suspicious. Besides which, he didn't have to tell her *everything*.

"My mother is a very strong-willed woman. Autocratic, in fact," Bain admitted as they took the turn toward the MacDonalds' place. He glanced over his shoulder to check on the horse. The stallion's great head bobbed as he docilely followed along behind them. "She still possesses great beauty, and can charm the kilt off a man when she so desires, yet she can also be cruel."

"Are you close to her?"

"Nae." Caitlin wouldn't believe the distance. For all her talk, she would have no way of truly comprehending his situation. "Though I think she loves me in her own fashion, my mother does not understand me, or what I would have of life."

"That's a common enough complaint," she said, her laughter soft and alluring. "My parents never understood me, either, especially when they realized I wanted to be an artist. Mother browbeat me into getting a degree in art education so I would always have teaching to fall back on. So, did your mother have plans for you?''

''Aye.''

''Doing what?''

''Exactly what I am doing. Seeing to our holdings.''

''And that was okay with you?'' Caitlin asked, sounding puzzled.

Bain clenched his jaw, took a deep breath and said, ''I had no choice in the matter.''

''Family duty, huh? I guess that's more ingrained into people who have castles and such as part of their heritage than it is to us Americans. Our culture is so much newer, and so is our thinking, I guess. However, there is something to be said for tradition, too.''

She was trying to make him feel better. Bain couldn't believe it—Caitlin Montgomery had the audacity to feel sorry for him! The knowledge irked him. Her cottage lay just ahead. Good. He would be glad to be rid of her. Why he'd ever allowed himself to get involved in such a personal discussion in the first place, he couldn't fathom!

Neither could he fathom the depth of his own anger.

Mere seconds later, they stood at her front door. His horse turned away from them and took an interest in nibbling at a patch of sweet grass. Giving them privacy? Bain grimaced.

Wondering what she was thinking now, he stared down at the comely lass with the wildfire hair and the come-hither eyes and felt his anger grow. He wanted brave Caitlin, and not merely for a night. He'd never before known a woman quite like her. One who would protect a crazy old man to whom she had no allegiance. One who would enter the darkness to steal back a brother she loved. If the truth be known, he'd never before really respected a woman he was attracted to. Not like this.

And in wanting Caitlin with every fiber of his being, he knew she was the one thing he could not allow himself. For he could not condemn her to hell. No mortal woman would or could meet his excessive expectations. 'Twas the story of his lonely life.

Would his destiny always be thus—to hunger after a wild and foolish fancy?

His resentment turned on Caitlin. She made him feel these things better left buried. She reminded him of his own discontent.

As if she could read his seething thoughts, she grew wide-eyed and said, "If you're not happy with your life, Bain, then do something about it."

The soft-spoken demand triggered wild and bitter emotions deep inside him.

So when she went on, adding, "This is almost the twenty-first century, you know, and we all can make our own choices—"

He chose to stop her blathering with a punishing kiss. One meant to frighten.

Unleashing his still-flourishing intensity, Bain forced Caitlin back against the cottage door and ground his mouth into hers. She was so soft and helpless against him, like a field mouse caught in the jaws of a hunting falcon. He could swallow her whole, this innocent little American.

She had no idea....

It truly seemed she didn't, for rather than wresting herself from his arms, ducking into her cottage and bolting the door against him, as would have been wise, Caitlin accepted his tongue with a cry that came from deep within, dropped her sketch pad to wind her arms about his neck, and pulled herself tight against him.

The circumstances rapidly altered.

His harsh intentions fell to naught.

Her power over him was such that he couldn't control himself, couldn't keep from turning what was meant to be punishment into an act of seduction. His hands skimmed her breasts, his palms enticed by the nipples that hardened beneath her sweater.

He sought her skin and found the entry to its smoothness easy, for she did not try to stop him. His hands shot up her sides and converged on the sweet flesh he sought. Scraps of lace were no deterrent. He merely pushed them aside and took her soft fullness in each hand. The catching of her breath, the whisper of his name crossing her lips, thrilled him.

And everywhere Caitlin touched him, intentionally or not, his body came alive. Meaning to show her how she stirred him, he spread his thighs and, abandoning her breasts for the moment, cupped her buttocks and pulled her into his need, which was hot and throbbing. He imagined the obstruction of garments between them gone, imagined burying himself deep within her. The friction and the heat made him shudder with arousal. And made his movements against her more intense.

Caitlin squirmed under the assault, but her reaction was one of pleasure, for, moaning, *she* deepened the kiss and clung to him as if she would never let him go.

If only that were true. If only she could hold on to him until she brought him back to the light he'd never known...

The thought was akin to a deluge of ice water sluicing through his veins, and he cooled instantly. He ignored the terrible ache between his thighs—and in the region of his heart—and, grabbing her shoulders, slammed her against the door. Then he backed away at arm's length. Eyes shadowed with fear and confusion, Caitlin stared up at him in openmouthed silence.

An uneasiness suddenly filled him. A perception of something being wrong. Senses alert, he tried to pinpoint the reason for his discontent, but the feeling was vague. Undefined. This woman muddled his senses, made him long for things that could not be.

She must be the danger he sensed, Bain told himself, wishing he was well and truly convinced.

"What's wrong?" Caitlin finally managed, without anger or recrimination in her tone.

Dare she feel sorry for him yet again?

"What's wrong is the absence of your good sense," he said tightly, everything else forgotten for the moment. "Beware of what animal instincts you stir in a man, lady," he warned. "Or next time you will not be let off so easily—I'll be taking more than a simple kiss."

Whistling for the stallion, he turned from her, but not before he saw the hurt and hunger in her expression. He fought his own reaction. Guilt was for a lesser man. One who had weaknesses.

He was allowed no such flaws. 'Twas not in his nature. He was, after all, his mother's only son, and had inherited her capacity for cruelty.

Wondering what had happened to Bain Morghue to make him so cruel at times, Caitlin watched him ride away without aiming so much as a look her way. Her hurt grew as her fright receded.

For a moment after he'd thrown her against the door, she'd relived the fear she experienced when Neil Howard threatened to kill her.

Bain had been angry, though she didn't know why.

That kiss had been meant to punish her. She'd known that, too, and yet she'd participated fully, and would have slept with him if he hadn't stopped. Thinking about the psychologist's claims that she might be attracted to the wrong sort of man, she picked up her sketchpad and slipped inside the cottage.

Without turning on the lights, she moved to the window. A movement outside caught her attention—Professor Abernathy disappearing behind the decorative hedge between the cottage and the manor. What was he doing, wandering about in the dark?

Caitlin focused out into the distance to find Bain. For a fleeting second, he reined in the stallion and glanced back, as if searching for her...and then horse and rider disappeared into the rising mists.

Caitlin was still suffering from the ache Bain had created inside her.

Pressing her forehead to the glass, she faced the fact that she was mooning over a man who had rejected her. Where was her self-respect? She turned from the window and felt for the light switch, and then was treated to yet another shock.

Someone had ransacked her things!

The covers on her bed were rumpled, her portfolio case, on the table near the fireplace, was unzipped, and some personal items that had been neatly arranged on the washstand were now strewn all over. Aghast, Caitlin stared at the proof of violation, wondering how the person had gotten in. The door had been locked, exactly as she'd left it, and all the windows seemed to be intact.

Her heart beat wildly as she turned in place, searching all the dark corners of the room. She was alone.

Thinking she'd better run to the manor and inform the MacDonalds, she stopped herself when she considered that the intruder might have been Bain. What if he had come looking for her earlier and, not finding her, had vented his frustration on her possessions?

Unlikely... but Caitlin knew she'd feel even more foolish if she made a fuss and the explanation was as simple as that.

Still stunned, she took another look around to see if anything had been stolen. Her jewelry was intact, as was the leather billfold with her airline tickets and traveler's checks. An even closer inspection finally revealed three missing items: a pillow cover from the bed, her hairbrush from the washstand, and a sketch of Bain that she'd left in the portfolio.

The inventory filled her with an even creepier feeling. What in the world would anyone want with such mundane items as a pillowcase and a hairbrush? And what about the sketch of Bain? She couldn't imagine why he himself would want it.

Then who?

Rubbing her arms to rid herself of a sudden chill, Caitlin remembered seeing Professor Abernathy in the dark, and wondered if he might have reason to want her spooked.

He could scare her half to death.

He had what he needed—a personal item, and one belonging to her quarters. The likeness of her protector was an added bonus, something he hoped to use later. For he had to find a weakness before engaging the Prince of Air and Darkness.

Still uncertain whether she, too, might not be after the treasure, he wanted her out of the way, wanted to eliminate both the threat of competition and the possibility that their lust-inspired bond might add to his enemy's strength. But while she wore the talisman, he could do nothing directly against her.

What he could do was make her wish she'd never left home. He could frighten her so badly that she would turn tail and run back to her native California.

He opened the ancient leather-bound volume, searching for an appropriate spell. After he'd taken care of her, he would start gathering his forces and make final preparations to do battle for what had to be the prize of all prizes.

CHAPTER SIX

After a near-sleepless night, Caitlin chose to say nothing about the weird theft to the MacDonalds over breakfast. She hated being suspicious of people she liked—especially Mary—and so was relieved when she finished and was able to make her excuses and leave.

But Professor Abernathy rushed outside after her, calling, "Caitlin, one moment!"

She gave the mild-looking professor a piercing glare.

"Mrs. Abernathy and I are off to see what's left of the Antonine Wall this morning, and we thought you might like to come."

Caitlin forced a polite smile to her lips. She couldn't be certain that the professor hadn't violated her quarters. "I've already made other plans," she fibbed.

"Really. What might you be up to today?"

Was he merely being friendly, or did the question have a sinister undercurrent?

"I thought I would wander through some of the nearby towns to soak up the local atmosphere." She started to turn away, but was stopped by a firm hand gripping her upper arm. Professor Abernathy frowned at her. "Think of the historical significance of the—"

Caitlin shrugged her arm free. "Thanks, but not today."

Before the professor could do anything to stop her, she hurried off to her rental car. Checking her rearview mirror, she noted that he was still standing in the same spot. Mrs. Abernathy joined him, and husband and wife huddled together. They seemed to be arguing, all the while staring after her.

Caitlin shook away a feeling of unease.

As good as her word, she drove straight through Droon to cruise through several other towns, but any local atmosphere remained elusive. Her mood remained distant, her mind preoccupied. She couldn't stop thinking about the strange things that had happened to her since she'd arrived in Scotland.

Having a car break down from some unknown cause the mechanic could only attribute to "fairy fire." Developing a relationship with a man no one but a crazy old shepherd seemed to have met. Being followed to the standing stones, then chased into the mystery man's arms. Finding her cottage ransacked...

What was going on? She felt as if she'd stepped into the Twilight Zone. If so, she was prepared to journey deeper into the uncharted territory.

After lunch, she found herself wandering through the woods and fields around Black Broch, sketchpad in hand. She couldn't stay away from the old ruins. Or from Bain.

She hopped across a narrow, babbling brook and made for a copse of trees that she hadn't before noticed. Stepping between the giant oaks—the place had the feel of a dark, primordial forest—Caitlin called up Bain's image. It was as clear to her as if he were standing directly before her. Windswept black hair. Midnight-blue eyes. Chiseled features. And a striking presence that bespoke power. Whether riding out of the mists, as she'd depicted him in her sketches, or threatening her with assault while naked but for his plaid, he made an unforgettable impression.

Then again, the potent effect he had on her was due in part to his temper. He always seemed to be angry about something, and, Caitlin suspected, not solely with her. Maybe his volatile makeup had to do with family obligations imposed on him by his authoritarian mother. He didn't seem to have much of a life.

He seemed so... isolated.

In his own way, he seemed to be cut off from the world as surely as her younger brother had been.

And maybe that was why Caitlin was never certain that she would see Bain Morghue again. Being with him stimulated her mentally, as well as physically and emotionally, but she couldn't look to any future with the elusive man, not even to the next day. Though he was clearly attracted to her, drawn to her in spite of himself, he made not even the simplest of commitments—a date.

Though Bain seemed to find her time and again, as if he knew her every move, Caitlin couldn't shake the fear that her midnight rider would slip away into the mists from which he had come, to disappear forever.

As if he were no more solid than a gossamer figment of her imagination...

Standing at the edge of a clearing, she looked upon the large, open area in the center—all the grass and flowers had been flattened. And the outer ring of undisturbed grass waved gently back and forth, though Caitlin could detect no wind. Goose bumps rose on her arms.

A fairy ring.

Impulse brought her to the very center, where beams of sunlight shafted through the trees. Her imagination began to work overtime. A fairy ring? Why not? What a wonderful place to create! But just as she thought that, she felt a chill breeze on her neck, and shivered. Something here felt forbidden....

She dismissed her fears and sank to the earth to sit cross-legged. She could almost hear the music, wild and alluring, could almost see the occupants of the invisible world prancing about her in a furious dance. Long ago, she'd read that a human's joining in the frenzied celebration could lead to a lifetime of captivity, the reveler being freed only if another, clever human came to the rescue.

She could almost see herself dancing with Bain.

Spirit lightened by that bizarre image—for she couldn't truly see Bain shaking a leg under any circumstances—she opened her sketchpad. Cocooning herself in the atmosphere of the place, she worked for what seemed like hours, her pencil untiring as it skimmed over page after page, leaving behind images that came straight from her subconscious—twining spirals, feral eyes, sharp faces, the inhabitants of the invisible world around her.

Eventually she grew sleepy. She was yawning and her eyes were watering, and at last she gave way and lay back against the crushed carpet, sketchpad safely at her side.

As if blown by tiny wings, the pages fluttered along with her lashes.

And then she gave over, allowing her eyes to close....

Bain's eyes shot open to greet a blazing fire in the small chamber where he'd drifted off some time before. Remembering the images that had danced through his head while he dozed, he was left unsettled. While he tried to make sense of this uneasy feeling, Ghillie Brown scurried to his side.

"Can I get ye food or drink, Laird?"

"Not now."

Fingers of dread walked up Bain's spine, disturbing him well and truly. A presage of something about to go wrong.

"But ye must eat. Must keep up yer strength if ye're to be properly vigilant."

Speaking of vigilance, Bain asked, "Where's the falcon?"

"Still stretching his wings, he be."

Bain didn't like it. Dusk grayed the room. "He should have returned by now."

Unless...

The pressure on his spine increased, and the skin along his neck crawled. Bain tuned in to the warning, but he could not fathom its source, and that fact made him still more anxious.

"I need to prepare."

Ghillie's eyes all but popped from his head, and the tufts of hair seemed to stand straight up from his ears. "Where be the trouble coming from?" he asked fearfully.

Bain didn't answer. Even if he was certain, he wouldn't be fool enough to test Ghillie's loyalties in this matter unless he had no other choice.

He stood prepared, naked in the midst of the standing stones, his flesh pale against the dark of night. Before him on the great horizontal rock altar lay the leather-bound volume, now closed, for he had no need to read words already committed to memory. His supplies were carefully laid out: dirk, chalices, burner and incense, hazel-wood wand, black iron pentacle, and a silver Celtic knot attached to a chain.

Wind swept through his hair and dew dampened his skin as he raised his hands and face to the full moon.

"I, Atholl, come to this sacred place of my own volition."

He solemnly intoned the magical name he'd chosen for himself, a name that would be secret from all but the Celtic gods...and the Prince of Air and Darkness. He would spit it in his enemy's face before vanquishing him.

"I once again dedicate my life to war and revenge."

His words rang ominously from standing stone to standing stone, the echo filling him with strength, making him imagine he spoke with their voices.

"I follow the ancient paths, and therefore ask that you place your all-encompassing power in my hands...."

He continued the self-initiation, anointing himself, laying the Celtic knot upon the pentacle and blessing it before hanging its chain around his neck. When metal met skin, he felt the power passing to him; his pulse quickened, and his blood soared. The wand in one hand, the dirk in the other, he made his plea.

"The gates between the worlds stand open this night. Behold, Scathach, O Shadowy One, She Who Strikes Fear... Behold, Caillech, Morrighan, Raise Up Your Legions. I beseech your aid...."

When he'd finished his chant to the dark faces of the ancient goddess, he turned counterclockwise within the rough circle of the stones, his dirk raised. Widdershins was always the direction for curses. Then he laid the hairbrush and pillowcase on the altar, smiling at the terror soon to be suffered by the uninitiated....

* * *

When Caitlin awoke, she felt chilled to the bone. A sough of wind floated on the air, carrying with it the distinct thrum of harp strings, the clarion call of flutes and the urgent tinkling of bells.

Hearing the sounds more clearly, Caitlin sat straight up and twisted around to see whence they came. The forest stared back at her, dense and unrevealing. And, though the sky above remained clear, a bright star shooting across the inky blackness, the ground surrounding her was carpeted with a swirling fog that seemed to be thickening, inching across the land like a serpent.

The musical sounds grew closer, more insistent, and joined with them was the baying of hounds.

"Hello, is someone there?" she called, still seeking the source.

Out of the mists in the distance stepped one horse, then another, with several more following. Their hooves were shod with silver, their heads were bridled with gold, and on their backs sat warriors and ladies dressed in fine embroidered, gilded and jeweled garments. They were led by a haughty-looking woman with silvered black hair, dressed in deepest blood red.

Caitlin stared openmouthed, certain the riders were all actors recreating some local historical event. But why hadn't the MacDonalds mentioned it? Or the local newspapers?

Horses and riders wound in and out of the mist, a pair of growling, snarling dogs trotting between the larger animals' legs. The procession was at first visible and then not. Though it was pitch-dark, a nimbus of light surrounded the courtly riders, making their forms glow with an ethereal brilliance. Behind them, a road cut through the forest, more spectral illumination offering Caitlin a clear view of a mighty black fortress with a tall, imposing tower. Black Broch?

While busy trying to make sense of this vision, Caitlin became aware of little skittering noises, and the *whish* of wings. Staring from the shadows were tiny, inhuman faces, terrible visages with sharp teeth and red eyes. She froze, afraid, especially when one of the shadowy things hissed at her and flew off like a moth toward the procession.

Then an eruption of sound, like hollow voices, made her glance toward the woman leader, who had spotted her and was pointing her out to her guard. Immediately two men turned their great mounts and spurred them into a charge. Their hounds followed, nipping at the flashing hooves. Caitlin flew to her feet and made a run for the trees on the other side of the clearing. But the trees drew no closer... exactly as if she were running in place. Her calves burned and her heart and lungs felt near to bursting, but the shelter of the forest continued to remain at an unreachable distance.

Thundering hooves directly behind her sent a chill straight up her spine. She whipped a glance over her shoulder, saw the bulging muscles of the destriers working as if they were moving in slow motion. Thick reddish vapor issued from the horses' flaring nostrils. One of the riders yelled a fierce war cry and held aloft an arm tattooed with a blue snake, brandishing a spear on which rested a bloody, half-rotted human head.

Bile rose in Caitlin's throat. The gap between her and her gruesome pursuers closed. Mists rose before her and just as suddenly parted, revealing a third warrior in black-and-gold armor.

She stumbled and fell to her knees. Pain jolted through her legs and back, and an invisible fist squeezed her chest. She didn't think she could rise, didn't imagine she could save herself. As the newest threat charged, however, she made the attempt. With a gasp, she shoved at the ground and lunged to her feet. Fog swirled around her ankles, sucking at her like insidious fingers.

The warriors were drawing closer, lethal weapons upraised.

The danger veered away from her, the riders and hounds converging to her right, the warrior in black and gold fighting the other two. Claymores clashed with the heavy ring of steel. Jerking to a stop, she stood there panting, wide-eyed, muscles quivering with exhaustion. But who—? She recognized the third man's mount, a powerful black stallion.

"Bain?" she gasped in wonder.

Had he really come to her rescue again? Glancing at her hand, she noted that the moonstone was glowing blue. But surely even he could not dispatch this particular danger as easily as he had the skinheads. These men were heavily armed. He was outnumbered. And the leader was dispatching more of her warriors!

Caitlin knew she had to help him. "Bain, watch your back!"

She raced toward the melee, cursing when her legs gave out and she almost fell again. Jaws dripping with foam, one of the hounds snarled and charged her.

Fear dissolved into anger—red, hot and seething.

With a screech of fury loud enough to split the heavens, Caitlin reached for the dog as it sailed toward her. Grabbing its ruff, she stopped it cold even as its jaws sank into her arm.

"How dare you!" She shook the animal and pitched it toward the troop's leader. "Go back where you came from, you cursed hound of hell!"

Belly low to the ground, the dog slunk off and, before her amazed eyes, melded with the mist.

"All of you!" Caitlin screamed, once more stumbling toward the armed warriors. While Bain fought valiantly, she didn't think he could hold off the reinforcements headed their way. She searched out the leader and yelled at the woman, "Leave us be!"

Hair flying around her mantled shoulders, the leader stared, eyes seeming to glow as deeply red as her garment. Careening to a stop once more, Caitlin locked gazes with the woman and refused to look away. But the physical exertion and mental stress had taken their toll. The image before her was wavering.

Caitlin sucked in the fetid night air and tried to hold on, but it was no use. Utterly exhausted, all her energies spent, she sank to her knees. The mist reached up to succor her, while constellations of stars whirled overhead. The next thing she knew, the black-and-gold-armored warrior was bending over her, mouthing her name.

She blinked, trying to focus on his voice, on his face. And then nothing...

"Caitlin."

She heard her name as if from a very great distance, and felt a hand on her arm shaking her.

"Open your eyes, lass," came an insistent voice filled with urgency, "so that I know you are well."

With a start, she obeyed, her eyes flicking open to meet a welcome sight. "Bain!" He was bending over her, his hand now stroking her face. "What happened?'' Heart pounding with remembrance of fear, she pushed herself into a sitting position and glanced around the field. It was empty, and all was still, threads of fog slinking along the ground the only movement. ''You managed to drive them off?''

''Drive who off?''

''The warriors. And the woman who led them.''

Suddenly she realized he was dressed in his usual dark pants, shirt and cape, rather than armor. And from what she could see of his moon-silvered expression, he appeared confused. And worried. His brow was furrowed, his mouth was a tight line, and his eyes steadily focused on her face.

She frowned. ''You didn't come to my rescue again?''

''I am here, am I not?''

''But the attackers . . . the hounds . . .''

''I think you have been dreaming.''

''A dream?'' she echoed, the sounds and images so clear in her mind that she could hardly believe it. ''But it was so vivid. The warriors and their ladies. The magnificent horses shod in silver. The hounds snapping at their heels. And the leader of the procession—a woman with silvered black hair, wearing bloodred garments . . .''

She imagined Bain stiffened, though he said nothing. He merely settled on the ground next to her.

A dream. She looked down at the ring's milky-white moonstone. This time the danger had been imagined, perhaps instigated by the incident of the day before, combined with the fairy-tale atmosphere of the clearing.

''This grove of trees must be enchanted.''

''I did say such existed,'' he reminded her.

She shuddered, then covered her inner turmoil by grousing, "But enchantment always seems so chilly."

"An easy problem to resolve."

He drew her to his side and draped his cape about her. She grew warm, not from the heaviness of the material, but from Bain's very closeness. His arm wrapped around her shoulders. His thigh snugged against hers. She felt as if she were melting inside, from the tips of her toes to the lobes of her ears, and every inch in between.

He filled every part of her.

Her heart thudded in her chest. She had reason to fear this closeness. To fear Bain. That he was dangerous, especially to her, would also help to explain the source of the dream, she supposed. As the gold-and-black warrior, he had personified power and danger. All afternoon she'd been thinking about him. About the strange things that had been happening to her. Now she had another incident to add to the list.

Though this one wasn't real, she reminded herself.

Caitlin worried about the line between reality and imagination blurring. She guessed Dr. Hoffman would have something to say about that. Ty's psychologist had been so certain she'd gotten deeply involved with Neil Howard because of her relationship with her brother, her need to rescue another lost soul. And hadn't she herself compared Bain's seclusion with the isolation Ty had experienced? Was she repeating her mistake yet again?

She didn't want to think so.

She wanted to think that life offered her more than some cockeyed, and perhaps fatal, attraction.

She wanted to think that she could truly fall in love.

And be loved for who she was.

"Tell me about the dream," Bain said.

At his urging, Caitlin did, leaving out nothing. And in the telling, the images became less real. Less frightening. More fanciful. Almost magical.

"A fairy rade," he pronounced when she had finished. "While doing your research, you must have read about the solemn processions of the nobility and knights of the invisible world."

She'd come across plenty of references to such before her trip, so he was undoubtedly correct.

"But it seems the rade became a wild hunt," Bain went on.

"A what?" Now *that* she hadn't heard of.

"Some people call fairies the unforgiven dead. When they ride about the countryside, looking for humans to sacrifice, it's called a wild hunt."

"Do they actually kill people?"

"More likely they frighten them to death...if you believe the legends."

"But we *are* talking about legends," stated Caitlin to reassure herself. Though that human head had looked very real.

"You must have come upon some mention of the wild hunt in your studies," Bain insisted. "You simply don't remember it."

"I'm sure you're right." Now she was beginning to feel a little silly. "My imagination was working overtime, I guess. And I was thinking about magic and fairies all afternoon. I even imagined this clearing to be a fairy ring."

Suddenly remembering her sketches, she pulled away from Bain to search for the sketchpad, and was relieved to find the darn thing within her reach. She was having an increasingly difficult time hanging on to her work!

"I was even drawing strange little faces when I fell asleep," she told Bain, pulling the sketchpad closer and settling down next to him again. Feral faces with pointed chins and ears, if not glowing red eyes.

He slipped his arm behind her; it was a band of steel supporting her back. She allowed herself the luxury of relaxing against him, of fantasizing some more. Sweet, inviting fantasies that stirred her to her very core.

"That explains it, then," Bain murmured, his lips brushing the top of her head. "And your subconscious probably called up the unseelie court—the hellions of the invisible world, rarely favorable to humans—because of the go-round you and Auld Sandy had with those hooligans yesterday."

Of course. She'd been reliving that incident, as well, before she fell asleep. Embarrassment flushed through her. "Thanks for not laughing."

"Dreams are powerful, not something to be made sport of."

He sounded serious, as if he really believed that.

"What kind of dreams do you have, Bain?"

When he didn't answer immediately, Caitlin was afraid she'd offended him.

Then he said, "A different life," and she didn't know whether or not she should be surprised.

"How so?"

"One with less demands. Or one with someone willing to share them."

Again she had the distinct impression of his isolation. His loneliness.

"We all want someone willing to share our problems," she said softly. "But to find that person, you have to share yourself."

With his free hand, he turned her face to his. Her heart bumped against her ribs when he murmured, "Perhaps I would be willing to share myself right now."

"I didn't mean physically."

Though her body thought otherwise. His flesh tempted hers through their layers of clothing, as if the garments presented no barrier.

"'Tis the closest two people can become."

Bain taunted her by sliding the length of his leg along hers. Caitlin squirmed inside as prickles of delight shot through her and her breath caught in her throat.

"No," she whispered, "it's not. Physical is easy." At least it normally was when two people were seriously attracted to one another. Nothing seemed to be easy with this man, though. "It's sharing what's inside you that's most difficult. And, ultimately, most rewarding."

His tempting mouth loomed closer as he said, "You're very wise for someone so very young."

"You're not so old yourself."

"You have no idea of how truly old I am."

Too much responsibility must surely have made him feel old before his time. Knowing he was about to kiss her, she said, "It's your life-style," stopping him cold, his lips mere centimeters away from mating with hers.

"Pardon?"

"All work, no play." From what she could see of his expression by moonlight, he was far too serious, even now. "You need fun in your life, Bain. You need to let go. To dare to be silly and carefree. You need to learn to love life."

He backed off. Slightly. "As you do?"

"I do... at least most of the time. I might not have reached all my goals," she said, thinking not only of her desire to develop her talents to the fullest, but also of the love she yearned to have for herself. "Yet. But I'll keep looking until I do. A part of me will never give up believing that somewhere, someday, I'll have everything I want."

His smile grew cynical. "Fame and wealth from your jewelry designs?"

"Happiness and someone to share it with," she countered indignantly, poking him in the chest. "See? We mortals all really want the same thing."

"Mortals," he echoed softly. The mocking smile intensified before it rapidly faded. His brow furrowed as he delved deep into her eyes, searching for some truth important to him. "Nae, Caitlin, you are an unusual lass, to be certain."

One who was getting all tangled up in his irresistible spell. "Except for having some talent as an artist, I'm as ordinary as they come."

"Not at all ordinary, or I wouldna want you so much."

Her heart thudded painfully. "You want me?" She'd thought so the night before. Then he'd pushed her away, leaving her angry and confused and empty.

"More than any lass I've ever known, pure heart."

And as he murmured the endearment, she knew he was telling her the truth. Then why *had* he rejected her? Out of fear? Of her? For her? Or for himself?

He stopped her wondering with a kiss. Deep, sensual, prying from her a wanton response. She tried to stay in control, tried to keep her mind separate from what their mouths were doing, what their bodies were yearning for, but she couldn't hang on to reality, not when the pleasure was so penetrating. The invisible world beckoned. A dream rather than a nightmare, this time. She and Bain whirling to music. A courting dance. And this only from a kiss. A touch. Two bodies fully clothed, stretching out on a magical bed of mist together.

He settled her close against the cradle of his arm, sheltered them both against the damp ground with his cape. "Perhaps you can teach me."

"I don't think you need lessons," she whispered, daring to tease him even now, when he was sending a sensual message along each and every one of her nerves. His hand was roaming, caressing her hip. Her waist. The flat of her stomach. She gasped, "You're doing just fine."

His laughter rumbled through her. "Nae, not this."

He sent his touch higher yet, so that her breast burned for more intimate contact. Without the boundaries of cloth . . . or of good sense.

"Teach me to be young again," he implored. "To appreciate life. To have hope."

"Wh-what?" It was difficult to pay attention to conversation at the moment, but she forced her muddled mind to focus. "That would be a tall order."

"But a challenge worthy of you, lady."

Still intensely aware of the touch of his beguiling fingers through her blouse, she could barely follow his words. Then he dipped his head, replacing his fingers with his warm, wet mouth, to sip and coax her through the thin material. She nearly lost herself.

"You will not take a dare?" he asked, his voice far cooler than his actions.

Again she had to force herself to concentrate on words. "A—a dare?" She wondered if she was up to it. After his rejection the day before...

Even as she thought that, he raised his head and straightened, slipping his hands back to safer positions at her waist and the small of her back. She couldn't help feeling disappointed, though she suspected he'd wanted to see just how much power he had over her.

"I dare you to teach me," he urged, tempting her.

She took a deep breath, trying to pull herself together. "Education takes patience and time," she said finally, keeping her tone light so that he wouldn't fathom how serious were her words. "Two qualities you sorely lack." Except when it came to lovemaking.

"I have time."

He said nothing about the patience part, Caitlin noted. "And when you disappear into the mist, I never know if I'll see you again."

Bain surprised her by rising suddenly and pulling her to her feet, though he kept an arm firmly around her waist. She remained tucked into his body under the cape.

"See me you shall," he assured her.

"When?"

"Tomorrow, early evening. Do you know of a town called Braemarton?"

"I think I drove through it this morning." Though she'd been so distracted, she didn't remember much about the place.

"Take the paved road out of town west a mile and you'll be coming to a fork. Keep to the right until you see the tents of the fair."

"What kind of fair?"

"One celebrating the old ways."

A date? "Like one of the medieval or Renaissance fairs we have in the States?" *He was actually making a date with her?*

"Aye, but more authentic."

"And you really will be there."

"My solemn word, lass."

Bain sealed the promise with a kiss that sent her blood singing through her veins. Suddenly, anything seemed possible. Caitlin clung to him for what was an eternity and yet no time at all. When he released her, she sensed his reluctance to let her go—far more satisfying than the inexplicable anger he'd displayed the night before.

But let her go he did, whistling for his steed, who'd been grazing nearby, while Caitlin fetched her sketchpad.

In one fluid movement, Bain mounted the stallion and, before she could protest, scooped Caitlin up and set her before him the way he had the night they met. No need to protest now. She wrapped her arms around his waist, laid her head on his chest and listened to his heart thundering in time with the hoofbeats all the way home.

Stopped before her cottage, he kissed her one last time, then released her. Her heart plummeted with her body. The moment her toes touched solid ground, she felt a sense of loss that only grew greater as, with a wave, Bain rode off as if the hounds of hell were on his heels.

"Tomorrow!" she called after him, disappointed and a bit anxious when he didn't acknowledge her.

She blinked, and he was gone, suddenly one with the night.

Leaving her with the uneasy feeling that the past hour with him had been all of a piece with her dream.

Not that she wanted to believe it. Not that she *would* believe it, she told herself firmly as she entered the cottage. Braemarton. Midafternoon. A fair. She would be there.

And Bain Morghue had better show!

Thinking to clean up before dinner, she removed her blouse, only to be puzzled by a rip in the sleeve. The vision of a hound sailing toward her and sinking its jaws into her arm flashed through her mind. But that was ridiculous, of course, for that had been part of her dream. Still, she stared at the jagged tear for a moment more before choosing to put it out of her mind.

After showering, she joined the others at the manor, but did no more than pick at her food. Her distraction did not go unnoticed. Alistair and the professor in particular seared her with meaningful looks, while Bridget muttered to herself in dire tones as she collected Caitlin's half-full plate.

"'Tis always the way it begins," the housekeeper mourned. "A bonny lass misplacin' her appetite, refusin' mortal company, losin' the use o' her tongue. Next ye'll be up an' disappearin' like the others."

"Bridget..." Alistair growled.

The housekeeper protested, "'Tis the truth! An' many a year has passed since the Guardian's appetite has been sated."

"This Guardian of yours sounds like a cannibal," Julian said dryly. "As for myself, I prefer a good piece of cooked lamb or beef." He turned to Caitlin. "What about you?"

"Uh-huh."

"I found a little pub that serves the best leg of lamb," he went on. "I thought we could take our evening meal there."

"Sure." Though she remembered agreeing to see him again, she couldn't remember why, exactly. "Sometime."

"Not sometime. Tomorrow."

"Tomorrow's impossible. I'm busy with research."

"But you've already agreed to it," Julian insisted. "The other day, over tea."

Had they made a specific date? Undoubtedly they had.

"An early dinner," she agreed, adding, "this is a working vacation for me." He needn't know that her evening's research would be done with another man.

Though Julian didn't appear altogether pleased, he inclined his head in a gentlemanly fashion. "Very well."

She excused herself from the table as Bridget brought out the dessert.

Less than an hour later, she lay in bed, sleepily anticipating what the next afternoon would bring. She'd barely closed her eyes and snuggled deep into her pillows when the noises began.

Wind wailing. Bushes thrashing. A howling in the distance.

She shifted restlessly, tried to force the sounds away.

Instead, they drew closer.

The windows rattled, and the very walls groaned, as if under some great weight. Sharp pings against the roof irritated her further. Great. An unexpected storm to keep her awake, just when she wanted to be especially well rested. Opening her eyes, she stared out the nearby window. Though the glass rattled within its panes, she could see no sign of a storm beyond.

It was as if the storm were within the house itself.

A creepy feeling shot through her, a feeling that grew more intense when her attention was drawn toward an ominous creaking and groaning. Either her eyes were deceiving her or the front door was bulging inward, as if made from rubber rather than wood!

Heart pounding, Caitlin shot straight up, ready to bolt. But to where?

Again she checked out the window in the direction of the manor. Not so much as a leaf of the hedges moved.

What was going on?

Then it came to her: a dream. She was asleep and having another damned dream! That was it. There could be no other explanation.

Breathing a sigh of relief, Caitlin muttered, "Oh, knock it off," before falling back to the mattress and pulling the pillow over her head to shut out the sounds.

CHAPTER SEVEN

Thinking she should have worn the silky dress she'd brought with her from home—Bain had never seen her in anything but casual clothing like the sweater and corduroy skirt she now wore—Caitlin was wondering if she had time to return to the bed-and-breakfast and change before driving out to Braemarton. But she was snapped to by Julian's piqued tone before she had a chance to decide.

"Are you certain you've been getting enough sleep?"

She looked at her dinner companion inquiringly. "Sleep?"

"You seem to be drifting off again." Obvious annoyance with her made his features sharper than usual. "I've asked you the same question twice now."

Caitlin flushed with embarrassment. "Sorry." Mostly because she hadn't found an excuse to cancel. A person who took her commitments seriously, she hadn't thought to let Julian down. She'd only agreed to dinner, after all. Unfortunately, Bain had been uppermost in her mind from the moment she awakened. "I am a little distracted."

"Yes, I noticed." He sliced into his leg of lamb with a vigor plainly spurred by irritation. "There must be something important on your mind."

"More like sensory overload," she said, remembering how Bain had made her nerves sing the night before.

"Sounds serious. Perhaps you'd care to tell me about it. Tell me about *something,* for heaven's sake," Julian said irritably, taking a bite of the meat.

A moment's unease skittered down her spine as she stared at him. "You know, I'm really enthusiastic about the research I've been doing for my jewelry designs." That certainly was true enough. "I get so caught up that it's enough to invoke sights and sounds from the past."

Not to mention from a world that didn't exist.

"You're altogether too focused on work. You need a break— This evening, for example."

"Actually, I enjoy my work tremendously," she said, torn between defiance and guilt.

He was silent for a moment, and he appeared anything but pleased as he swallowed another mouthful of food. Caitlin looked away, studying the dark paneled walls and old-fashioned carved wooden bar of the pub, which was spilling over with happy customers. It really was a nice place, and she wished she could be more appreciative.

Finally Julian asked, "So what's on your busy schedule today?"

Uncomfortable with the direction the conversation was taking, she replied carefully, "Learning more about the old ways." She still couldn't bring herself to tell anyone about Bain.

"A trip to the library?"

"Something a bit more lively." Before he could ask what, Caitlin turned the tables on him. "What about you? Why are you vacationing in Scotland? Looking for antiques to sell in your shop?"

"I always keep an eye out for new pieces, of course, but I'm actually doing some research of my own. Family-tree sort of thing."

She was surprised. "You don't look Scottish."

"The connection is far, far in the past." He indicated her food, which she'd barely touched. "You don't seem to be enjoying your meal. Would you like something else?"

"No. This is delicious."

Spearing a piece of lamb herself, Caitlin concentrated on eating, a difficult task when she was so pumped about the coming evening. She was anticipating the excitement of spending some real time with Bain when she realized she'd tuned Julian out again.

She tuned back in as he said, "Caitlin, I realize we haven't known each other but for a few days, but I've grown very fond of you." His expression softened as he took her hand and stared down at the falcon-and-moonstone ring. "Soon you'll be off to America, and I'll be back to London. I shall miss you. Until then, I would like to propose we spend as much time together as possible. I would be willing to help you with your research...."

Uh-oh, she hadn't been ready for this one. "I don't think that would be wise." She determinedly slipped her hand free from his possessive grip.

"Then you don't return the affection?"

Never one to hurt another's feelings if she could help it, Caitlin avoided answering directly. "I'm...sort of...involved with someone." Or so she hoped. "It wouldn't be fair to you."

"So, you do have a young man waiting for you back home."

He stared at her steadily, his mouth pulled straight in an unattractive line, but she neither confirmed nor denied his speculation.

Instead, she said, "I hope you don't feel that I've led you on."

"No, of course not."

But the pique was there again, making Caitlin wonder if Julian was used to a woman turning down the offer of his company. He really was attractive, but even if she wasn't falling for Bain Morghue, she wasn't certain she would have considered forming a closer bond with Julian.

Something about him put her off.

She gave him an uneasy smile and suffered through the next half hour. When they left the pub and went to their separate cars, she felt a weight lift from her shoulders. She only hoped Julian had gotten the message and would reconcile himself to her disinterest. If not, things would become uncomfortable at the Mac-Donalds'.

The drive into the westering sun soothed her. This time she really saw the land she crossed—rolling moorland laced with rippling streams and scarred by peat bogs. The road snaked along gaps in hills that wound up and down, mile after mile, eventually taking her through several coal-mining villages. By the time she arrived at Braemarton, she'd put everything out of her mind but Bain and their date.

The town itself was similar to Droon, most of the buildings whitewashed and thatch-roofed. As she drove through the town's center, with its few tourist establishments, she looked for signs indicating a fair nearby. Finding none, she hoped Bain hadn't been mistaken, and she fought a mounting disappointment as she traversed the road out of town.

Shortly after passing the fork, however, her tension dissipated, for she spotted a costumed couple walking by the side of the road. The woman was wearing a sleeveless red tunic and cape, while the man wore a thigh-length blue tunic, a yellow cloak, and leather footgear tied around his legs.

A few seconds later, Caitlin found herself in a strath. The large valley between blazing green hillocks was dotted with several colorful tents. Parking her car amid dozens of others, she worried that her heavy gold sweater and brown skirt would be conspicuous, since the area was bustling with costumed people.

Spotting a few who wore street clothes made her feel better, and she ignored the suspicion that some of the more finely costumed fairgoers seemed somewhat familiar—a reminder of the fairy rade dream.

Where to find Bain?

Wandering around the edge of the crowd, Caitlin realized she hadn't considered how large the event might be, and regretted his not having been more specific about a meeting spot. She needn't have worried, however. She was standing near the orange-and-yellow-striped refreshment tent when Bain came up behind her and murmured, "Have you a thirst for ale, lady?"

Caitlin couldn't help herself—she grinned from ear to ear at him. This was the first time she'd seen him before dusk fell, and she couldn't stop staring. He was so handsome, she could hardly believe he was real. Today he wore an acorn-brown velvet tunic shirt that resembled a costume and yet was uniquely Bain. Around his neck he'd added a torque, a bronze neck ring formed of two rods twisted together and thickened at the ends. Even in trousers and riding boots, he looked right at home with the mix of people dressed in everything from the simplest of ancient-looking garments to more elaborate medieval gear.

"The ale can wait. First I want to see *everything*."

His enigmatic "Perhaps you shall" puzzled her, but he didn't give her time to question him.

A pie seller balancing a tray on his head passed by as Bain cupped her elbow and led her farther into the open glen. Its perimeter was sporadically dotted with hawthorn and hazel, oak and elder. Other merchants hawked their wares, everything from jewelry to good-luck charms to birds in cages. Bain bought a wreath of dried flowers and ribbons from a barefoot girl enveloped in a cloak. The huge rectangular plaid pinned at the right shoulder was especially popular with the fairgoers.

Placing the crown on Caitlin's head, Bain brushed his fingers along her cheek, sending a flutter straight to her heart.

"Thank you," she said, mesmerized by his eyes, which today held a violet hue. "It's beautiful."

"As are you."

He lowered his head and kissed her, his very gentleness making her ache for so much more. She wanted his arms around her, his body pressing into hers. The attraction she felt for him was like a thirst that she couldn't quench.

Feeling oddly shy when he retreated, she glanced around. "What a shame this fair isn't advertised."

"No need. Those who participate every year know about it. 'Tis celebrating Beltane," he explained, "marking the cycle of light, the beginning of the summer season."

"Beltane... May Day?"

"The same."

"But that's tomorrow."

"The Celts began their celebrations at midnight." Bain took her arm and led her on. "The Eve of Beltane is a dangerous, bewitched time," he warned her.

Wondering if he was serious or was actually teasing her, she said, "If you believe in that sort of thing."

"Aye." His eyebrows raised as he stared down at her. "And even if you don't."

Caitlin still considered *him* dangerous to her, emotionally, if no longer physically, and his words roused in her a small thrill of alarm. She remembered his saying the fair celebrated the old ways, and wondered how connected *he* was to the past. Considering the way he dressed, and his preferred mode of transportation, she guessed the connection might be pretty strong.

"The Celts considered May a month of sexual freedom in honor of the Great Mother and the Horned God of the woodlands," Bain was telling her. "Couples contracted trial marriages of a year and a day, at which time they could separate if they were not happy."

His intent expression flooded her with an uncomfortable warmth, and her warning signals went up. The conversation was beginning to feel all too personal. She was happy merely to be spending time with Bain, and she didn't want to ruin it with speculation about the future. She looked around for a distraction, and found it in a pair of artists working nearby under an elder tree.

"Look, they're painting tattoos on people," she said, grabbing Bain's hand and dragging him closer. A woman was having her bare arm decorated, a man his entire chest. She gave Bain a sly glance. "You would look pretty good with one of those."

He raised a challenging eyebrow. "I think not, lady."

"And I thought you wanted to learn to have fun. So loosen up already."

Grumbling, he gave over, and Caitlin watched with fascination as intricate lines of blue paint covered half his cheek and the side of his neck.

"The elaborate twining of the design is a guard against the evil eye or curses," the artist told them as he put the finishing touches on his work.

"Sometimes there is no protection against a curse," Bain returned. "If the one who casts it is powerful enough."

Caitlin fought the sudden chill that invaded her at his unexpected response. Bain was far from a whimsical man. He made the statement as if he really believed it...as if he had firsthand experience with the predicament.

But when he gave her a wry smile and asked, "Satisfied, lady?" she relaxed.

The atmosphere of the fair was making her imagination work overtime.

"Very pretty," she told him teasingly.

They spent the next hour or so wandering about, inspecting merchants' booths and observing people of all ages enjoying themselves in participatory events. Caitlin bought a small book, and then she and Bain watched several raucous men and a woman who were engaged in an archery contest. To the noisy delight of the crowd, the woman won. And in a nearby mud hole, two men dressed in peasant garb tried to catch a squealing hog. Both opponents ended up covered with mud from head to toe, and the hog trotted off triumphantly.

Next they stopped for a few minutes near an elaborate miniature stage, where an old Celtic myth was being reenacted with marionettes.

"They look so lifelike," she whispered to Bain. "Like real little people." Creepy little people, she thought, staring at one with a pointed chin and a red cast to his eyes.

"Perhaps they are. Anything can happen on Beltane Eve," he reminded her. "Occupants of the invisible world canna help but be drawn to the festivities."

She didn't know whether she liked that or not. Shivering, she thought of the proud ladies and bloodthirsty warriors, the tiny faces she'd glimpsed in the shadows with their sharp teeth and bad attitudes. She moved closer, and was relieved when she saw fine strings attached to human hands manipulating the detailed puppets. She smiled at her own silliness. Perhaps she should place boundaries on that imagination of hers!

As they continued along, a jester made both Caitlin and Bain laugh aloud, and then strolling musicians had her humming happily.

"I would remember you always," Bain murmured as they approached a pastel portrait artist just finishing with a pleased customer.

Flustered, Caitlin tried to protest, "Me pose for another artist? I don't know."

"Loosen up, lady." Bain echoed her own words and laughed at her indignant expression.

She gracefully gave way. "If you insist."

"The name's Tam, bonny lass," the artist told her. His huge grin accentuated the slight slant of his eyes. "'Twill be pure pleasure to capture your likeness."

When he moved to reset his easel, Tam's long, dark blond hair parted, giving Caitlin a glimpse of the tip of a pointy ear. She also noticed that, rather than a sketchpad or a piece of vellum, the artist used handmade rag paper. Composed of animal hair and wood fiber, it was one of the oldest forms of art paper still being used in the present.

"Will ye be posing in what ye've got on, or in traditional dress?" Tam asked.

"Traditional," Bain answered for her.

He also chose the costume she was to wear for the sitting, which he rented from a middle-aged woman who ran a concession in a booth across the way. Caitlin loved the russet colored tunic with tiny bells on its fringed sleeves. To that, he added a forest-green overdress to keep her warm, and a beautiful brooch that looked like real gold filigree. The brooch's heart-shaped stone seemed to be a ruby, though she couldn't imagine anyone investing so much money in costume pieces that could easily disappear.

"This gown be perfect with yer hair and eyes, lass," the stocky proprietress said when Caitlin emerged, transformed, from the curtained alcove. She reached up and straightened the dried flowers in Caitlin's hair. "Made fer ye, it could be."

"Green is my favorite color."

The woman laughed, exhibiting a mouthful of rotting teeth. It seemed she'd never heard of modern dentistry. "'Tis good, since green honors the Earth Mother." She whispered, "Children conceived this night are blessed wi' the luck o' the Scots."

And Caitlin was getting the distinct feeling that sexual activity was one of the favorite ways the lusty old ones had had of celebrating Beltane Eve. Heat flushed through her when she met Bain's expectant gaze. She imagined he could read her mind. That he *knew* she was wondering what it would be like to make love with him.

And she knew that he wanted her.

Blood coursed through her as she brushed by him and took her seat. She posed self-consciously, both because the easel was being turned on her as model rather than artist and because Bain never seemed to take his eyes off her. A myriad of emotions played havoc with her thoughts as sunlight deserted the strath and Tam paused in his work to put flame to the half-dozen torches he'd already set out in a semicircle around the stool—no electricity here.

How had she fallen under Bain's spell so quickly, so thoroughly? She'd never before considered sleeping with a man she'd known for less than a week, but that was what she'd almost done two nights before. He'd been the one to stop them, not she. Despite all indications that Bain was a man to fear, she'd convinced herself he was no Neil. What if she was wrong? Not that she believed he would hurt her physically, as Neil had threatened to. But wounds to the heart and soul were far slower to heal than were those to the body.

And Bain wasn't an easy man, no matter how accommodating he might seem at the moment.

Yet each time their eyes met, each time they touched, each time she heard the thrilling timbre of his voice, Caitlin knew she desired Bain Morghue more than any man she'd ever met. This sweet desire went beyond the physical longing that made her breasts and belly ache for his touch. It went far deeper, and Caitlin was beginning to realize she was willing to risk her heart and soul to be with him in every way.

An irrational act of bravery?

Or was she a woman falling truly, deeply, madly, in love for the very first time in her life?

"Finished," Tam said, just as she became impatient with all the sitting. He waved Bain closer. "What think ye, Laird?"

Laird? So he knew Bain. Caitlin was inordinately pleased.

"As fine a likeness as I've seen you create, Tam."

Rounding the easel, Caitlin stared openmouthed. The woman staring back at her was, indeed, a perfect facsimile of her... and yet not. The woman Tam had captured was vibrant and earthy and...magical somehow. To Caitlin's chagrin, she also appeared to be absurdly lovesick.

"The model makes all the difference," Tam was saying. "She's the bonniest lass of them all."

Had Bain commissioned Tam to do portraits of other women, Caitlin wondered, or was he speaking in general terms?

"Aye, the bonniest and the bravest," Bain was saying. "Hold it for me, if you will, Tam. I wouldna want such a masterpiece harmed by this night's work." He took her elbow and moved off.

She immediately protested. "Wait, my clothes—"

"Shall be returned." He smoothed the loose sleeve of the tunic, his fingers biting into her flesh through the material in an intimate caress. "This is yours now, as well."

"Bain, no," Caitlin protested, knowing the outfit couldn't have been inexpensive. "I mean, I love it, but it's too much—"

He smothered her protest with a warm and sensual kiss. As his tongue seduced hers, Caitlin flushed with desire and knew that she was well and truly under Bain's spell. She could deny him nothing.

"Sometimes, lass," he growled softly, "you speak too freely."

"That's because you don't talk enough," she said in mock irritation.

"My stomach speaks loudly. For food."

He steered her in the direction of the refreshment tent. Instead of thinning due to the lateness of the hour, the crowd had multiplied, as if the festivities were only now gathering momentum. Lamps and torches dotted the glen, and Caitlin had the oddest sensation of being in some time warp. It was as if she'd somehow stepped back into the past.

Or into that invisible world Bain was always talking about.

He startled her out of those thoughts by asking, "What would you have me speak of?"

"You!" she said without hesitation. "You're a cryptogram of a man, Bain Morghue. And while I enjoy the challenge of a worthwhile puzzle, I expect the reward of being able to solve it in the end."

His hand grew stiff on her elbow, and his voice had a definite edge when he stated, "You know what you need to know."

Damn! He was withdrawing before her very eyes. "You're wrong, Bain. I don't know nearly enough."

"More could put you in danger, brave Caitlin, and I'll be having none of that."

"What danger?" When he didn't answer, she said, "All right, then, how about your distant past? Let's go all the way back to your formative years. Surely knowing about your childhood is safe enough."

"Aye, one's childhood *should* be safe," he agreed.

But the way he said it, his tone mournful, made her believe that his hadn't been. Thinking of Ty, of the way she'd sheltered her younger brother and of her own emotions concerning his withdrawal and recovery, she chose not to press Bain.

As they approached the refreshment tent, they passed a man draped in a plaid and playing the bagpipes. His stunning, porcelain-skinned, carrot-topped companion was doing a Highland sword dance. Stopping to watch for a moment, Bain tossed several coins into the dancer's basket and received a smile in return, a smile so bold and sultry that Caitlin imagined they knew each other. Her furrowed brow was smoothed when Bain took her arm and ran his cheek along her hair, convincing her she was the only woman who had his interest now.

"I thought you were hungry and in a hurry to eat," she murmured, leading him off.

"I am," he said, his long, hot gaze making Caitlin feel as if she were to be the main course.

She was distracted from erotic speculation by a pair of noisy warriors jostling the crowd. They wore their shoulder-length reddish-blond hair tied on both sides, and their mustaches were so long, the stringy tips hung nearly to their chests. Both sat upon horses whose only tack consisted of crude bridles and woven cloths. One of the men was drinking from a horn-shaped vessel, and his raised arm was embellished by a huge blue snake tattoo.

Caitlin froze, struck by a sudden thrill of fear.

"Is something wrong?" asked Bain.

She swallowed and told herself that many men could have snake tattoos. The twining serpent was a common Celtic motif. "Some of these fairgoers get pretty realistic."

Bain merely raised his eyebrows.

When one of the horses snorted, she decided to ask about Raven. "Your horse isn't around here somewhere, is he?"

"Nae, I sent him home."

"Alone?"

"He knows the way."

Thinking this was surely a tale, she narrowed her gaze at her date. "And how will you get home?" She expected him to say he'd let her take him.

"My steed knows my whistle. He will find us."

Did Bain plan to sweep her away from the fair on horseback? Caitlin wondered, happier than she remembered being in a very long time.

The food at the refreshment tent also seemed reminiscent of the ancient past. Dishes of boiled pork, roast ox and game were advertised on crudely printed signs, as well as bowls of curds and milk and horns of ale and mead. Though Caitlin opted for a more familiar roasted turkey leg in the way of food, she gladly tried the mead and soon felt the effects of the sweet liquor made from honey and spices.

Her tongue grew loose.

"About that childhood..." she began, ignoring her earlier reservations about pressing him. She wanted to know everything about Bain. "Was it so terrible?"

He sat across a planked table from her. "It felt endless."

"That's a pretty common experience. When you're young, a week takes forever to go by. But when you get old, the years seem to fly. Or so I've been told."

"But most children have at least one parent to count on. To spend time with."

"Yours weren't around?"

He shook his head and swallowed a mouthful of food. "Not often enough. Servants raised me. Other jealous children in the castle were always playing tricks on me, until I didn't want to be with them, either."

It sounded as if he'd been a very lonely child, Caitlin thought, her heart going out to him.

"Your parents were doing what? Traveling on the Continent?" Wasn't that what wealthy couples did?

"My mother had great responsibilities running her and Father's various interests."

"Hmm...a career woman." No doubt one who wanted to take it slower now that she was older, and relied on Bain to shoulder all that responsibility for her. "What about your father?"

"Too often involved in military maneuvers."

"An army man?"

"He belonged to a select group of fighters."

"A mercenary then."

"Of a sort," Bain agreed, taking a swig of ale. "His death was a waste. He wasn't even in a real battle at the time, merely a silly skirmish. I wanted to avenge him, but my mother stopped me. I was too young, she said, and told me to wait at least until my voice deepened."

Having dealt with loss, albeit a temporary one, Caitlin empathized. "So you don't have many memories of him."

"Nae, but the ones I do have are stronger than you can know. Father had a half brother, born out of wedlock—an angry young man, who wanted everything that belonged to Father. Thinking he could take over with the correct leverage, he kidnapped me before my father died and held me for ransom."

"How horrible."

Bain nodded. "I was alone and frightened and thought I would be left to rot in that hole. I thought I would never hear my mother's lovely voice in song again. I don't remember how long I was held...an eternity to a small boy. I only remember the day Father broke into the narrow chamber where I had been caged. He looked so grand and powerful, wearing his plaid and weapons. When he took me in his arms, there were tears in his eyes. A dangerous and fearless man, unafraid to cry for his son...that's how I shall always remember him.''

As she stared at Bain's face, seeing the open emotion etched there, Caitlin's own eyes stung. She found his hand and grasped it tightly. ''He must have loved you very much.''

''Aye. And I him, especially after that day when he gave up his other duties to come for me.'' His free hand wound around hers. ''Does it satisfy you to know this, brave Caitlin?''

She wouldn't be satisfied until she knew everything about Bain. ''It's a start. A *good* start,'' she emphasized, locking on to his gaze.

Something invisible, indefinable and invincible sparked between them. He'd told her so little, and yet so much. Admitting to the kidnapping had to have been difficult for a man with so much strength and pride. He'd opened himself to her, and unless she was a terrible judge of character, that wasn't something Bain Morghue did often.

First, he had to trust.

Caitlin wanted to tell him he could trust her, that she wouldn't let him down, that she would never leave him alone for even one day. Then she realized the gravity of her thoughts, the consequences should she change her mind tomorrow and choose to return home. She wasn't ready for this. A serious commitment. And with a man who had seemed unready to commit himself to so much as a date until today. She was way ahead of herself. Ahead of them.

She was in love.

The thought elated her and frightened her and plagued her. What to do? Eat. She stared at her half-stripped turkey leg and suddenly realized she was ravenous and yet without appetite. Was this what being in love was like? Feeling all of a jumble? Uncertain?

If so, then she was alone in her torment, for Bain seemed to be having no trouble gulping down his food, swilling down his ale.

Giving him a filthy look that he missed altogether—he was too busy filling his mouth—Caitlin picked at the remaining turkey flesh until Bain finished, heaved a great sigh and leaned on his elbows, looking utterly contented.

"Swine," she muttered.

"What?"

"I was merely thinking about those two men who were wrestled into the mud by that hog," she fibbed.

"'Twas amusing," he conceded, looking at her carefully, as if he didn't trust her explanation.

"I'm done. What next?"

"Something to lift your spirits. Come."

He held out his hand. For a moment, Caitlin thought to refuse him. Then she caught the soft glint in his mesmerizing eyes. A glint meant for her alone. Ah, she was lost in his eyes.

Before she could get her wits together, Bain swept her across the grounds and pulled her into a smaller tent whose floor was a bed of furs. Their steps were hushed as they entered. Everywhere she looked, shadows warred with pools of light. Candles on the floor, on tables and even set in higher niches made layer upon layer of hanging silks shimmer and glow as they undulated delicately with each slight draft of air. Antique mirrors suspended everywhere reflected images back and forth, giving Caitlin the feel of infinity. Of intricate illusion.

"Where are we?" she asked.

"A timeless place. One where the past, present and future come together without warring."

Puzzled, Caitlin drew closer to a central table. Its scarred surface was of varied woods inlaid with Celtic designs. Two chairs opposed each other, and in the table's center lay a large pouch of bloodred velvet.

"Seeking truths, are ye?" came a woman's lilting voice that seemed to surround them.

Seeking the source, Caitlin whirled so fast that the wreath flipped from her hair. "Who..."

Her question faded into nothingness when she realized she was alone.

CHAPTER EIGHT

Caitlin's heart thudded strangely. "Bain?" How had he disappeared so fast? Why had he left her? And where had he gone?

"He is one with the night," the disembodied voice answered cryptically, as if its owner had read her mind. "He knows what needs be."

A tall, bold, shadowy form inched through a maze of silken banners. Caitlin's mouth went dry, and she felt absurd for being afraid. She was at a fair, for heaven's sake, and this woman was merely a . . .

"But ye need to see the future more clearly, do ye not?"

A fortune-teller!

Caitlin forced herself to take a long gulp of air as the woman stepped into the tent's open central area. She blinked in surprise. Rather than being tall and regal, as her shadow had first indicated, the woman was aged and cronelike, wreathed in black, long silver hair hanging loose to her waist, back hunched, her face so lined it might have seen centuries rather than decades pass. Hard eyes on Caitlin, she held out a gnarled hand to indicate that her visitor should sit.

Obeying, Caitlin paused when her foot caught on something—the wreath that had spilled from her hair. She picked up the ring of dried flowers and ribbons and hung it from the back of her chair. The fortune-teller took the seat opposite her and retrieved a velvet bag. Without preamble, she tossed the contents on the table.

Celtic divination sticks!

The two dozen flat sticks were crudely hand carved of wood, and a third of them lay faceup, their cryptic Ogham runes inscribed in what Caitlin imagined to be the red of blood.

The crone inspected a gathering of three sticks closest to Caitlin. "Mor—the Sea—indicates restlessness," she began, her voice now sounding as aged and rough-edged as she looked. "That ye be using travel to escape yer problems."

A bit startled, Caitlin told herself the woman must have recognized her accent as American and figured she was on vacation. Everyone had problems they wanted to get away from, right?

"Perhaps even from danger," the fortune-teller added, sending a tiny chill down Caitlin's spine. She moved on to the second stick. "Coll—Hazel Wood— here there be a creative fire strengthened by rising desire."

Lucky guess, Caitlin decided, though she was shifting in her chair now.

"Ivy." The crone indicated the third in the grouping. "Things may not be what they seem. Ye must search below the surface for the truth."

"What truth?" Caitlin asked, trying to free herself, to believe in the magic. To fully enjoy an experience that would surely stay with her forever.

"Whatever truth ye be presently looking for."

Bain?

"But Straif Reversed presents the obstacle." She tapped the lone revealed stick to Caitlin's left. "The

Blackthorn is a trickster in human disguise. Beware of him and his advice, for he means ye ill.''

Caitlin's mouth went dry. Could this represent whoever had chased her over the sea lochs? And ransacked her cottage? She couldn't stop herself from asking, "Someone I know?"

The crone's oddly pale eyes were piercing. "Of a certainty." She then inspected the stick almost directly opposite. "Ah, the sign of Gift and Security. Ye be both strong and generous. Giving of yerself. Capable of deep relationships. This stands ye in good stead in yer struggle."

"With whom? The trickster?"

"Nae. He cares for naught but himself. Beware, lass, for he be of a great danger to ye."

The warning got to her, sent a jolt of fear racing down her spine. And, to her mounting dismay, the crone's next statement was no more reassuring.

"Necessity Reversed." She pointed to the stick closest to Caitlin. "Ye must avoid quick decisions. Think carefully on making a commitment."

Her head had been filled with thoughts of commitment since she'd become involved with Bain. Odd how the fortune-teller kept hitting on her fears and concerns so accurately. The old woman was fingering the last of the revealed sticks, which lay in the midst of the others. Her lined face pulled into a frown, she was mumbling to herself and shaking her head.

"What?" Caitlin asked, unsure she really wanted to know.

"Not good. Not good," the crone intoned. "Ancestral Property Reversed. A problem with inheritance . . . a break with family."

That could mean her leaving California permanently. But it sounded more serious. "I'm not expecting any inheritance."

"But ye can effect one. Disastrously," the fortune-teller predicted, looking fierce.

Again her thoughts snapped to Bain. He was the one with the family responsibilities. Could she have such an affect on him? Separating him from what was left of *his* family? His mother?

Caitlin eyed a stick tucked under the last. No symbol: "What about this one?" she asked, daring to flip it over herself. Blank.

"Wyrd." The crone's voice cracked as she explained, "Fate. Something ye canna know, and I canna foretell. Only fate can decide the issue."

So, in the end, she could heed all the old woman's warnings and fate would still have the final word.

Caitlin realized what she was thinking, the stock she was putting in some fortune-teller's predictions, just because she'd been lucky enough to hit on a few half-truths.

This was a game, for heaven's sake, one she was supposed to enjoy. Bain had expected her to.

"Is that it?"

"'Tis enough." The piercing eyes locked with hers. "Ye donna believe ... but ye shall."

Caitlin popped out of her chair. "What do I owe you?" she asked before realizing she had left her wallet in her skirt pocket.

The gnarled fingers waved her toward the entrance. "'Tis done."

"Thank you," Caitlin muttered, rushing out through the hanging silks. She'd barely set foot outside the tent, had barely breathed one sigh of fresh night air, before she realized she'd left her wreath dangling from the chair's back. "Darn!"

Retracing her footsteps, Caitlin was surprised when the fortune-teller was nowhere to be seen. Both she and the sticks were gone. She wouldn't have bet the old woman could move so fast. Wreath in hand, she was about to leave when she heard a rustling behind her. She whipped around, expecting to see the crone. No one.

A glimpse of movement caught her eye. A reflection repeated in the various hanging mirrors. A vision of a beautiful woman with long, silvered black hair, dressed in a bloodred gown, whose expression was threatening. And chillingly familiar.

The leader of the fairy rade?

Caitlin whipped around to face the other woman, but no one stood behind her. And when she rechecked the mirrors, the vivid images had vanished. Pulse dancing crazily, she flew out of the tent . . . and straight into Bain's arms.

"Whoa! Running from me?"

Caitlin grasped him and was relieved to find him solid and warm and real. "From myself," she said, her heart thudding. Panic turned to another, more erotic, form of excitement. "From my imagination." She said no more, and Bain silently led her off, deeper into the heart of the glen. Tension thickened the very blood that pulsed in her veins.

"'Tis almost midnight," he whispered.

Caitlin set the wreath in her hair. "The real start of Beltane. I assume there'll be some sort of special celebration to mark the occasion."

"The ancient rituals will be observed," he agreed.

People were milling about all around them, coming from every direction, heading toward the center of the valley. Only a few wore modern street dress. Many had donned garb representative of the Middle Ages. But most individuals looked as if they were trying to appear authentically Celtic.

Several young men who wore bronze helmets and carried oblong shields nearly as long as they were tall flirted with young women in tunics and plaids secured at the shoulder. Caitlin remembered all the inferences of lusty activity associated with the celebration and wondered, amused, if that part of the tradition would be reenacted, as well.

Just then, Bain slid a warm palm along her back, grasped her waist and tucked her neatly into his side.

Each step, each movement, each touch, increased her awareness of him. She licked her lips, tried to breathe deeply, attempted to find some safe reality within the enchantment of the evening. For Bain had been correct about Beltane Eve being bewitching and dangerous. She was falling under the spell of the ancient holiday—she was already under *his* spell—caring not for the consequences in the days to come.

All she knew was that she wanted Bain, that she ached for him, that she was sick with longing for him, as if the Eve itself had woven a spell from which she could not free herself.

Did not want to free herself.

A strange and strident sound rang out through the strath. When she looked up at Bain questioningly, he said, "A war horn, blown for battles."

"Are we to fight, then?"

"Perhaps with each other." He lifted a brow. "But I promise you a very pleasant encounter."

Caught up in his light mood, Caitlin laughed as he moved her to the very center of activity, where workers had just finished stacking wood into two huge piles. A half-dozen people with torches surrounded each pile. The horn blew again, and they set flame to the two great bonfires. Together, the conflagrations lit the night sky.

Then the ground trembled, and a wild, rhythmic noise made Caitlin whip out of Bain's grasp and fly around in alarm. "What in the world—?"

A thundering herd of panicked cattle split the crowd in two. Wrapping an arm around her waist, Bain lifted Caitlin off her feet to get her out of the stampede's path. Wild-looking men, their light hair helmeted with bronze, brought up the rear. Another man rode in a wooden chariot, his hair slicked in spikes with some pale substance, his mustache braided. He was nearly naked, wearing little more than his tattoos—parallel lines on his sides and arms, a stripe down his nose and across his cheeks—which looked real, rather than painted on.

As he rode between the bonfires, people began to follow, running and laughing.

Bain bent down so that his lips were close enough to her ear that she might hear. "'Tis considered good luck," he explained. "The smoke of the bonfires is purifying."

The next thing she knew, wild musical notes struck the air—from lutes and harps, flutes and drums. The sounds were enticing and urgent. The noisy people between the bonfires separated into two lines, men on one side, women on the other. They began to sway and tap their feet in time to the music, beginning a traditional dance.

Bain urged Caitlin forward, to her surprise, for it seemed he meant for them to join the promenade. She remembered having thought he wouldn't know how to dance. He let her go at the end of the line.

"Lady," he said, bowing at the waist and backing away from her.

More people were joining them, including other musicians. The melody grew fuller, and Caitlin found herself easily copying the simple steps. The lines surged forward. Met. Partners clasped hands and circled each other. Swept away by the carefree, almost frantic mood, she laughed up into Bain's face. *He* had never looked more open. Happier.

The two lines separated, snaked through each other, dancers touching hands and changing partners all the way down the line and circling back again. Caitlin was grinning, enjoying herself thoroughly, when a hand fastened on to hers and jerked her to a stop.

Hard.

Startled, Caitlin looked up into the frowning face of Professor Abernathy. What in the world was he doing there? She was immediately on edge.

"Come with me now. It's urgent."

She read his lips instead of actually hearing him over the cacophony surrounding them. Why was his expression so contorted? The fire blazing hellishly behind him gave the normally mild-looking man a demonic look. And why was he trying to pull her off to one side?

An unnamed fear swept through her, and a frantic Caitlin plucked her arm away as if freeing herself from the devil. She ran to catch up to her place in line, looking over her shoulder until the professor was swallowed whole by the surging crowd. Her hands were clammy and cold as she passed from partner to partner. When she met again with Bain, her relief was intense. He whirled her in a circle, then stopped when she gripped his velvet tunic with both hands and sagged against his chest.

"Let's get out of here," she pleaded.

Sensing her urgency, he led her away from the celebration, deeper into the heart of the strath. Sounds followed, cutting through the crisp, clear night. She glanced over her shoulder, saw other couples slipping away, also, no doubt for secret trysts in the dark.

Intimacy was the last thing on her mind at the moment. Her heart was pounding, and her mind was whirling. Had the professor followed her, or had his appearance merely been a coincidence? The crone's predictions echoed in her head. She'd spoken of a trickster, someone who would give her bad advice and mean her ill. He'd wanted her to leave with him. Why?

No one could harm her while she was with such a powerful man as Bain Morghue, Caitlin told herself, especially not some elderly professor.

He waited until they'd crossed the glen and reached a sheltered cove of trees before demanding, "Now tell me what's troubling you."

Caitlin suddenly felt foolish. "I'm not sure. I mean, strange things have been happening to me for days...and then the fortune-teller going on about someone trying to fool me...and then the professor showing up here tonight."

"What professor?" Bain asked, stiffening.

"An American. He and his wife are staying at the MacDonalds', too."

Bain relaxed. "He undoubtedly heard about the festivities from some local and came for the experience. Perhaps he was worried about your being alone."

"I'd like to believe that. But he's taken more than a friendly interest in my comings and goings in the past few days." She gazed around the sheltered area. No one had followed. They were completely alone. "And he tried to drag me off from the dance tonight."

Bain tightened his arms around her. "And that was enough to frighten you?"

"That and being chased along the sea lochs, and then my cottage being ransacked—"

"What?" Bain thundered. "Someone broke into your quarters? Why did you not tell me?"

"Whoever it was only took a brush and a pillow-case," she said, defensive about not telling anyone because she was feeling even more foolish.

Bain muttered something she didn't understand. A Gaelic curse, perhaps?

Some of the tension drained out of her, and she was warmed by the depth of his concern. "Putting a curse on someone?"

"And if I am?" he asked stiffly. "You find this amusing?"

Part of her did... and part of her took the suggestion very seriously.

"I'm relieved," she assured him. "I really was frightened, but you make me feel better. Safe."

"I want nothing untoward to happen to you, my brave heart."

So now she was *his?* She smiled, even though he sounded worried, as if he had reason, and Caitlin found herself reassuring him. "I'm fine now. I'm with you."

At the moment, she couldn't conceive of ever having feared Bain Morghue. He was holding her as if she were precious to him. As if he would never let her go. As if he meant to keep her safe forever.

His voice was a rough whisper against the velvet of the night. "If anything happened to you because of me..."

Before she could ask him what he meant by that—how could her knowing him be dangerous?—he freed her just enough to kiss her. The mating of their mouths was more than a kiss, Caitlin thought as the blood sang wildly through her veins.

He meant to brand her.

To devour her whole.

She gloried in the feel of his hard warrior's body against hers, of the tongue invading her mouth in a rhythm that made her light-headed. The celebratory sounds from the middle of the glen grew less distinct as she became lost to his power. Alive. She felt so alive. Every inch of her being. Of her soul.

Or *their* soul, one and the same, she thought hazily, drunk on the sweetness of his kiss. Two hearts beat as one. Why not two souls?

The images that thought conjured...

The emotions.

The fear.

No, not fear. Fire. Heat quickly flashed through her as his hands slipped to her breasts. He tested their fullness, drew his thumbs across the already hardened nipples. When his hands moved again, she cried out, the protest lost in his mouth, which never left hers. He worked at her dress and tunic, opened her flesh to the cool night air and the strong imprint of his fingers as they memorized every inch of her. She should be cold, but she was burning with desire.

She wanted him. Needed him.

And now she would have him.

Her senses unnaturally heightened as he stripped her of the garment, she blamed the mead and the promised enchantment of Beltane for making her feel so wanton. The bells of her tunic tinkled beguilingly as they floated to the ground, leaving her one with nature.

Breaking the kiss, she helped Bain remove his own clothing. They were panting, their hands tangling together in the garments, their frustrated laughter blooming into a symphony of luscious sound, as they completed the task. Though Caitlin had only glimpses of Bain's musculature where the moon shot beams through breaks in the leafy bower overhead, she knew he was magnificent. Male beauty personified.

Touching, memorizing, anticipating... She was well and truly enchanted.

His skin slicked against her breasts as he lowered himself before her. On the way down, he kissed, nipped, tasted. Caitlin hung suspended between heaven and earth, between the moon and the stars. One arm behind her back balancing her, Bain surged forward and down so that she floated lightly to their bedding of discarded garments, with him following to rest over her.

Around them a cloying fog was rising—a living, vital entity sliding along their limbs—though she would swear the conditions were all wrong for such a turn in weather. Magic. That was it. Everything about the night was bewitched, even the unexpected haze.

A thin veil of moist air surrounded Bain lovingly as he found her, stroked her, prepared to slide into her. Appropriate, for hadn't he appeared to her out of the mists in the first place?

Caitlin arched and, with a cry of triumph, met his thrust. His power impaled her, filled her, made her careen toward the edge of the known universe. He held her there, suspended in time, as if the centuries would pass and he would not tire of loving her. Each time she reached for the stars, her fingers met fairy dust that scattered with the winds.

She dug them into his flesh and whispered, "Bain, help me. Please . . . help me."

With a groan, he complied, shifting and driving into her until nothing could keep her from ecstasy.

Behind her lids, the inhabitants of the invisible world danced in a circle, trampling the grass into the earth. She joined them, whirling, gliding, leaping. Frenzied. Unable to stop on her own.

Strong arms pulled her back to reality and Bain's all-too-real flesh. He leaned back and cradled her against his chest as the fog reached up and devoured them both.

CHAPTER NINE

Caitlin lay in Bain's arms for some time before her heartbeat returned to its normal cadence. She listened to his breathing and to the stirring of leaves above them in the wind. Nature's poetry. The air smelled of spring grass and moss and salty mist. She felt at one with nature, as if she had just made love with a woodland god.

Bain.

Though he was quite human, thank goodness. Real flesh and blood. She snuggled her cheek against his warm chest, feeling more sheltered and loved than ever before in her life. The cool night couldn't chill the embers of the fire banked at her core. Things had changed between them, no matter how short the time they'd known each other. Their relationship was about to take a new direction, she thought, loving the way his breath feathered her hair.

She stirred and stretched. "That was wonderful."

"Mmm…" He sighed and slid a hand along her bare hip. "Aye, now we've done it," he said, his tone holding a presage of doom.

And making Caitlin stiffen. "Done it?" she echoed.

"Finally sated our lust." He rearranged the cloak that lay over them. "I suppose 'twas unavoidable. But let us not think on the problem you pose until the morrow."

Her emotions having risen like a dancer to the sound of the harp, they were poised beneath the very surface of her skin. Hurt tingled along every nerve ending. "You think all we've shared is lust?" She lifted her head. "And that I'm a problem?"

Instead of answering, he tried to press her closer.

Caitlin pushed him away and rose to her elbow. "I gave myself of my own free will, Bain. I won't try to tie you down or make you commit yourself...if that's what you're worried about." Even though she loved him.

"We are bound whether we will it or no, lass. Twice, thrice bound now." His voice sounded troubled as he stroked her arm. "You dinna understand."

"Of course I don't understand. You're never straight with me." Didn't he realize how insecure that made her feel? "We didn't just sate our lust, Bain, we made love. At least I did," she stated, a lump growing in her throat, a vise squeezing her heart. "I was touched to my very soul."

He sighed again. "All the worse for you, lass. Now you'll never be free."

Wounded by his disappointing response, Caitlin said, "I am not listening to any more of your gloom and doom." She'd thought he'd gotten beyond that. She'd foolishly thought he might even return some of her feeling for him. She scrambled to her feet and tore her tunic and dress out from under him. The bells' tinkling no longer sounded charming. "I had a glorious experience, and you're not going to ruin it!"

"Caitlin," He said, his voice soft, as he sat up and watched her struggle with the unfamiliar clothing. "And what do you think you're about to do?"

"Leave. You may be great at the physical part of making love, but you're rotten when it comes to the rest!"

"Caitlin, wait!"

He rose to his feet, and she hoped he would truly try to stop her, to mend the ache his cavalier attitude caused. Even in the dim light, she could appreciate his naked strength. Dried leaves clinging to his tousled hair, he truly resembled a god of the forest.

Or a demon lover who'd finished a woodsy seduction.

When he said nothing, merely continued to stare at her implacably, she scurried away from him, shouting, "From now on, you stay away from me!"

Enough of his mysterious ways.

Caitlin glanced toward the tents of the fair, darkened now, the crowd having dispersed. She wasn't going back to get her clothing, didn't care if she lost her sweater and skirt. Fog still cloaked the deserted area. She glanced about nervously, well and truly spooked now. Someone could be waiting to jump her, and she wouldn't see him until he was already upon her. Her shoes crunched on gravel as she hurried to the car. Her hand was on the door when she realized she didn't have her wallet or keys.

"Damn!"

Well, she'd walk to the B and B if she had to. But then she glanced in the vehicle's window and spotted what appeared to be her sweater. She tried the handle—the door opened easily. The sweater and skirt she'd worn to the fair lay folded neatly on the passenger seat. How did they get there? she wondered with a thrill of unease.

Sliding into the car, she felt the pockets of the clothing, quickly locating her keys and wallet. Even the book she'd purchased was lying safely beneath the pile in a paper bag.

Strange.

But she was too hurt and angry to think long upon yet another miraculous incident. She just wanted to put as much distance as possible between herself and Bain Morghue! Inserting the ignition key, she started the car and spun its wheels pulling out into the road. With difficulty, she swallowed her tears and drove faster than she should have through the fog. She had trusted him and had given herself, but Bain hadn't been able to trust and give back. At least not enough to whisper sweet words in her ear after making love. She hadn't required promises, merely a loving touch.

But then, they'd probably never be able to have anything close to a normal, natural relationship.

Caitlin tried to ignore the little voice inside her that suggested Bain wouldn't be half as interesting if he were a run-of-the-mill kind of guy. Was her interest in the unusual—the unknown that was the inspiration for her magical jewelry—also the reason she felt attracted to troubled men? Because they were so unusual, they piqued her curiosity?

Taking a curve too fast, Caitlin decided she was sick and tired of digging into her psyche about men who attracted her.

She was sick and tired of the frequent, bothersome fog.

She was even sick and tired of Scotland.

When she turned into the MacDonalds' drive and parked near her cottage, she breathed a deep sigh of relief. She'd left a light on inside, the window glowed dimly through the mist. She found the key and was about to place it in the lock when she heard furtive movement behind her.

Heart pounding, she whirled around. "Wh-who's there?"

The tall form of a man loomed in the fog.

"Caitlin?"

Bain's voice! What was he doing here? How had he beaten her home? The horse. He'd taken a shortcut.

Now her pulse quickened for reasons other than fear, but she hardened herself against a too-easy seduction. "Go away. I don't want to talk to you."

"There's no need to talk," he said smoothly. "Give me the ring."

"Why? Do you want to break up?" she asked sarcastically.

As if he'd ever committed himself to her. She twisted the intricate falcon on her finger, thinking she ought to slide it off and throw it at him, not even knowing what stopped her.

"Give me the ring, Caitlin. You don't need it anymore."

His voice was soft and mesmerizing. Coaxing. Not a trace of anger. He should be mad as a hornet, after the way she'd left. So why wasn't he? Caitlin narrowed her eyes against the swirling mist, barely able to glimpse the pale oval of his face.

"Give me the ring."

His voice sounded hollow, stilted. And he remained some distance away. Which was also unlike him. Usually he came close enough to breathe down her neck.

Fingers still twisting the ring, she fought the growing impulse to slide it from her finger. "Is the danger over?"

"It's gone. Give me the ring, Caitlin!" he commanded for the fourth time.

How very insistent. That was more like the Bain she knew. Caitlin started to free herself of his token . . . but then a loud call suddenly split the air from somewhere in back of her.

"Herbert Abernathy!" the professor's wife shouted. The open door of the American couple's thatch-roofed cottage spilled light into the gloom. "Where are you? It's the middle of the night!"

Caitlin glanced behind her for only a second before returning her attention to Bain.

But he was gone.

She stared into the empty fog, slowly regaining her faculties, her brain feeling as fuzzy as if she'd been hypnotized.

This time her hand shook as she inserted the key and let herself into the cottage, making certain not only the door but the windows, too, were bolted. She switched on more lights and gazed about the room, brooding on Bain's hollow voice and the distance he'd kept from her. Had she really been speaking with him?

Or had it been the trickster?

She thought of Professor Abernathy and the hard way he'd clutched her arm at the fair earlier. And just now his wife had been calling him. Could the professor have been pretending to be Bain? To get the ring?

Dead tired, she headed for bed, jumping when she caught sight of the stranger in the mirror. Her tousled hair, her swollen lips, her disheveled green gown, made her look like some earthy, lusty wench from another age. And her eyes seemed huge and startled and strangely wise ... from seeing things few other humans had?

"Wise, phooey!" she snapped.

A smart woman wouldn't have fallen in love with the likes of Bain Morghue.

* * *

He was furious! Wandering through the mist, he picked up stray rocks and threw them as hard as he could at the smirking darkness. Ineffectual as it was, the violent action nevertheless felt good. He was acting like a little boy, he knew, but he was too irate to care that he debased himself.

Nothing was going the way he'd planned! He couldn't scare the stupid chit into fleeing back to her own country with either dreams of fairy rades or nightmares of eerie storms. She wouldn't give up the ring that protected her and connected her to his enemy, either. He had used his most commanding tone, and she had still managed to disobey. She was strong and contrary for such a little thing.

Her strength posed a more terrible problem. If his enemy joined with such a mortal as Caitlin Montgomery, if his enemy made full use of her fawning love, he could well be impossible to defeat.

He had to find a way. . . .

Meanwhile, he would take care of the incompetent spy who'd been sniffing about on his trail. That one would be sorry he had ever stuck his nose where it didn't belong.

Not feeling sociable when she awakened the next morning, Caitlin didn't go to the manor house for breakfast. Instead, she boiled water for tea in the small pot in her cottage and ate some shortbread cookies she'd purchased in Droon.

Working on her designs, she spent an hour or so trying not to think about Bain and whether she'd overreacted to their tryst the night before. When she tired of drawing, she leafed through the small book she'd purchased at the fair, an illustrated guide to the local area's history. She started at the beginning, reading about the Bronze Age and continuing through the eighteenth-century war against England led by Bonnie Prince Charlie. She paused upon finding a footnote mentioning the name MacBain. The clan had lived on land near Droon some centuries before.

MacBain?

Could Bain be descended from that family? Had the clan inspired his name? Knowing she shouldn't care, Caitlin tore through the rest of the history book, but couldn't find another reference. In frustration, she decided to talk to Alistair MacDonald. His extensive library would surely offer more information.

Unfortunately, the owner of the bed-and-breakfast was busy with Julian when Caitlin came in. Glancing into the study, she saw him pointing out the swords he had hanging on the walls above his bookshelves.

"I have three eighteenth-century sabers but only one claymore," said Alistair.

With some difficulty, he reached up to lift down the heavy sword. A wicked-looking weapon, it bore dark opaque stones, rather than jewels, in its pommel. And the twining metal of its hilt wasn't half as bright or as beautifully crafted as Bain's.

"Very nice." Julian ran a finger along the sword's blade. "I came upon a genuine claymore myself yesterday. It cost more than I wanted to pay, considering the hilt was in sorry condition."

Alistair shrugged. "But what can you expect, if 'tis old and authentic? And you can have the stones replaced, the metal polished, the blade sharpened."

"The blade was already quite sharp." Then Julian noticed their observer. "Oh." His smile was wide, but his eyes were cool. "Good day, Caitlin. Aren't we the late riser?"

She expected him to go on, to say something about staying out the night before with her boyfriend. She was certain he still resented her for not finding him as attractive as he seemed to find her.

When he didn't continue, she said, "Actually, I've been up for hours. I had tea and cookies for breakfast while working in my cottage."

"How industrious of you."

She didn't like Julian's smooth, knowing tone. And she only wanted to ask Alistair some questions, not to get into some lengthy three-way conversation.

"Thank you for letting me look at that claymore," Julian said, surprising her by taking his leave. "It gives me an idea of how I could refinish one of my own."

"Glad to have been of help," said Alistair, still holding the sword.

Caitlin waited to be certain Julian was gone, then asked, "Could I talk to you for a few minutes?"

Laying the claymore across his desk, her host motioned to a chair. "Take a seat."

She plopped down and showed him the history book she'd been reading. "This footnote says that the MacBains once lived on land near Droon. But it doesn't say what happened to them."

Alistair merely raised his brows.

"I mean, they're no longer here," she went on. "They're not listed on any of the clan maps I've seen. Something must have happened to them."

Alistair glanced at a shelf, then rose to take a large book from it. "They were dispersed, driven out of this area by the English. Decimated, actually. That happened to many clans after Bonnie Prince Charlie, though there be some reason for it with the MacBains, if you ask me."

"A reason to be decimated?" How unusual for a Scotsman to side with the English.

He opened the book and raked his finger down a page. "Aye, here it is—the last recorded laird of the MacBains had a regiment of English soldiers buried alive on the grounds of Black Broch. An excessively cruel man."

"So the legend is true?" Caitlin asked, a chill creeping up her spine. What else had she encountered that was based on actual happenings?

"Of course, the English took terrible revenge. They executed the laird, and all the followers they could capture. Who knows what happened to the survivors?"

"Why didn't you tell me this before?" she complained.

He frowned. "You didna ask."

Even as he spoke, Caitlin realized she'd never mentioned the tales she'd heard in Droon, partly because she hadn't wanted to be tempted into bringing up Bain himself. She smiled sheepishly. "Right, I didn't ask you about the clan." Or every detail of the ruins' history. "And I discussed the regiment story with some of the townspeople. Do you know if the MacBains still own Black Broch?"

"I once tried to look up the deed—not an easy task with hundreds of years to account for. But I believe the latest owner is some corporation."

That didn't help. She'd already surmised that his operating through a company might be the reason no one had heard of Bain Morghue.

Alistair closed the book and gave her a thunderous look. "You aren't still hanging about that place, are you?"

He sounded as tense as he looked, and she thought it best to keep her counsel. "I've gone there a few times to sketch."

"Best keep your distance entirely."

"So I've been told. I suppose there's some myth about the ghosts of the murdered soldiers haunting the broch."

"The ground itself is full of blood. The MacBains were cursed with a feud that went back generations. It started with two brothers, one misbegot—"

"Illegitimate?"

"Aye. And he was always wanting the leadership and recognition himself. The two branches of the family warred for years, decades and centuries, the misbegotten line using any means, fair or foul. That line finally won, and was in power when the regiment of soldiers was buried."

"And then the laird and his followers were executed," Caitlin murmured thoughtfully. "Foul means finally got them their just desserts."

Bain had mentioned that his father had had an angry half brother who once kidnapped him. But that had happened in recent times, not generations ago. Could Bain be descended from the dark side of the family? she wondered. He had also said that his mother could be cruel.

Alistair rose to replace the large book on the shelves. He surprised Caitlin by taking down another. She stared at the aged-looking black cover embossed with gold ink. The words *Celtic* and *Faerie* stood out in the long title.

"More myths and legends?"

He leafed through densely printed pages. "I've been doing research since the morning you said a rider had brought you back to your cottage on horseback." His eyes flicked over her, then returned to the book. "Of course, Bridget is superstitious, as are many of the old country families. To people like them, Black Broch is an evil place guarded by a demonic caretaker who watches over a treasure. The gold is cursed by the devil and means death to anyone who tries to find it."

She nodded. "Gold in the cairn."

"Wouldna be surprised if archaeologists turned up such a find someday. Might be jewelry, as well as ancient Celtic armor, such as helmets and breastplates." He paused while riffling the pages. "Hmm, here it is— a fairy legend that could pertain to Black Broch."

"It *could* pertain to it?"

"The legend doesn't specify Black Broch in particular, but it bears much similarity to the story of the Guardian and the gold." He moved closer to peruse the tiny print. "Once upon a time, it seems, the queen of the Tuatha Sidhe took a liking to a mortal man, a chieftain who was a great warrior. She stole him away." Alistair gazed at her. "You know that fairies weren't always pretty little Disney characters?"

"I'm aware of that."

"When you study fairy lore, you find hundreds of varieties, both evil and good, unseelie and seelie. Some had wings, some did not. Some were tiny, others were human-sized."

"Like the Tuatha Sidhe." The Gaelic words were pronounced *toona shee*. "And some of the supposedly good fairies could be pretty bad themselves," Caitlin pointed out.

Alistair nodded.

Instinctively feeling Alistair was building up to something, Caitlin was growing impatient. "What about the queen who stole away a mortal lover?"

"Right, the queen. Let's call her Mab or Morrighan. Her British and Irish names are easier."

Morrighan...similar to Morghue?

"She is also called the Queen of Air and Darkness," Alistair continued. "So Morrighan and the chieftain had a son, a man who was only half-mortal, able to visit, if not live, in the invisible world. The Prince of Air and Darkness was condemned to guard the entrance to the place, and was given a suit of golden armor that granted him both immortality and invincibility."

"That does sound like the guardian Bridget was talking about." A warrior dressed in gold and black...like the one in her dream of the fairy rade.

"This guardian was also a demon lover of sorts. Seems he seduced women from time to time, carried them off body and soul."

His words shot chills up Caitlin's spine as she realized that her body and soul were Bain's...and he did not want them.

"But what can you expect of a man who was probably tortured and unhappy?" remarked Alistair.

"Someone who didn't belong to either world." Bain? Was that why he acted as if she were doomed?

Alistair slammed the book shut, making her jerk in her seat. He fixed her with a cold eye. "Strangely enough, there *have* been many suicides—or murders— connected with Black Broch."

She swallowed. "Women?"

"Aye, mostly. No one knows what happened to Janet Drummond, and at least two other women leaped off the promontory...or were pushed. Then a young woman was found raving in the courtyard one winter, wearing only her night shift. She died a few days later.''

Caitlin asked, ''These deaths you're talking about actually happened, right? You didn't read about them in that book?''

''They were real. The mad woman in her nightshift died in 1931, according to some newspaper clippings I found.'' He picked up the claymore, examining its blade. ''You'd best be careful, or you might become the next statistic.''

The way he was staring at her, unsmiling and grim, gave her the heebie-jeebies.

She rose. ''Thanks for the information.''

''No more questions?''

''You answered them all, and then some.'' Except the one she couldn't ask—who was Bain Morghue? ''I think I'll be going.''

As she left, Alistair stood and picked up the claymore, giving the air a couple of vicious pokes with the sharp tip. Already nervous, Caitlin couldn't help wondering if he could mimic voices.

Was Alistair MacDonald the trickster the fortune-teller had warned her about?

Fortune-tellers. Basing her opinions on the reading of divination sticks was almost as ridiculous as believing in fairy tales, Caitlin had decided by the time she'd had a light supper of fish and chips in Droon that evening.

She was altogether too tense. She needed to unwind and relax. For the first time since arriving in Scotland, she wished she had access to a television. The Mac-Donalds didn't own one. They thought travelers should enjoy the country's ambience without the drivel of electronic entertainment. But a silly sitcom or two would have helped her forget about Bain Morghue and the strange fancies she'd entertained since meeting him.

Not that she could see him as an evil man who lured women to their deaths. Not in the farthest reaches of her imagination. He wasn't *that* cruel. She'd told him to stay away from her and he had. He hadn't chased her down or strong-armed her the way crazy Neil Howard had.

Catching a flash of colored light through a pub window as she passed, Caitlin peered in. But the group of men clustered about the bar were watching a soccer game, not anything humorous.

Truly desperate for diversion on the dark drive back to the MacDonalds', she ran over the plot of one of her favorite old comedies. Suddenly the headlights of the car lit on something pale in the ditch as she drove by, something that looked like a shirt or jacket.

Odd. Country roads in Scotland weren't litter-strewn like American highways. Perhaps someone had lost something. Nearly at the driveway of the B and B, she stopped, glanced behind her at the empty expanse, then reversed the vehicle. Parking the car on the narrow shoulder, she kept the lights on and got out to investigate. She soon realized the jacket she'd seen was being worn by someone . . . a man who lay very still.

Caitlin recognized the stocky figure, the meaty back, the silver hair. "Professor Abernathy?"

Good Lord, had he had a heart attack?

"Professor?" she called again, running toward him, hoping she remembered her CPR training.

Facedown, he didn't so much as twitch a muscle as she knelt beside him. The back of his jacket was stained with a rusty substance, and she felt something sticky as she turned him over. His eyes stared up, slightly glazed over.

Speechless, she saw his chest, matted and caked with blood. A deep wound gaped at her.

Horrified, Caitlin inched backward, struggled to her feet and ran for the car.

Professor Abernathy had been murdered!

CHAPTER TEN

Professor Abernathy had been killed by the thrust of a powerful sword.

So said the authorities who questioned Caitlin, the other guests and the B and B owners and staff at the manor house. Constables searched both manor house and cottages. A violent crime of this sort hadn't been committed in the area for decades, and the police wanted to be thorough.

"I tell you it was the city crazies," Alistair complained angrily after several hours of questioning. "You could have done something about them long ago."

Sergeant Cooke, a big man with a sandy mustache, shook his head and sighed. "And what could we have done? 'Tisn't the Middle Ages—you canna drive someone out of your territory just because you want to."

A constable added, "You'll have to turn over your sword collection, Mr. MacDonald. The weapons must be checked against the entry wound by a forensic laboratory."

Which only incensed Alistair the more. "*I'm* to be considered a suspect?" His rugged face was flushed. "An honest, taxpaying citizen? While those city punks go free?"

Mary, her eyes reddened by tears, placed a calming hand on her husband's arm. "Now, Alistair. 'Tis only procedure."

Julian nodded a sober agreement. Caitlin had noted that he had seemed truly shocked by the murder and had been supportive toward the MacDonalds and helpful with the police.

"Not that we won't be looking for those city crazies," said Sergeant Cooke. "Meanwhile, you will all stay in this vicinity and be available for further questioning... except for Mrs. Abernathy, of course."

The widow had become hysterical at the sight of her husband's body. Though sedated now, she was still weeping quietly. She insisted she wanted to pack up and take a taxi to Glasgow, expensive though that would be. She had friends to stay with in the city, and could no longer stand the sight of the cottage. Since the police seemed certain that a small, fiftyish woman wouldn't be strong enough to run a man through with a broadsword, they had no problem with her leaving the vicinity.

Professor Abernathy's wound had been deep and massive, and Caitlin's imagination was hard at work— to her chagrin. She'd told Bain the professor had been annoying her. Surely he wouldn't have taken that as a sign to "protect" her with his claymore. He hadn't acted as if he wanted to do real violence to the skinheads who'd frightened her.

Still, she couldn't help but be worried. Doubly so, as she realized she might be withholding evidence concerning a prime suspect. She nearly sagged with relief when the police indicated that the interrogation was over.

"I'm sorry about your husband," she told Mrs. Abernathy as they left the manor house together.

Mrs. Abernathy wiped her red nose. "Thank you, dear."

"I can help you pack, if you want."

"That's not necessary. I'm only taking a few things. Mary will send the rest on to Glasgow." She gazed at Caitlin with soft brown eyes. "Don't blame yourself, dear. It wasn't your fault."

Not *her* fault? "What do you mean?"

"Herbert insisted there was a prowler sneaking about your cottage at night," Mrs. Abernathy explained. "He took it upon himself to investigate. He was concerned because you were a young woman on your own."

Caitlin focused on the prowler part. "He saw someone outside my cottage?" Bain?

"Herbert was out snooping for hours the past two evenings."

Which explained why Mrs. Abernathy had been calling for her husband the night before.

"I didn't like it," the older woman admitted. "I was afraid he'd get himself into trouble. But I never suspected the prowler would be a murderer." She sniffed, wiping her nose again. "If I were you, I'd leave this place immediately. You're welcome to come to Glasgow with me."

Her emotions mixed, Caitlin seethed with questions.

Had the Professor died trying to protect her?

Then who had mimicked Bain's voice in the fog?

Was Alistair indeed the trickster?

Or Julian?

Surely *that* person was the one who'd murdered Professor Abernathy. Not Bain.

"Caitlin? Would you like to come to Glasgow?" Mrs. Abernathy repeated.

Caitlin thought she probably *should* leave. And she supposed she could talk the authorities into allowing her to do so. But she needed to have a long talk with Bain.

"I can't go yet."

"I shall be very frightened for you."

Poor Mrs. Abernathy! She took the woman's hand. "Please don't worry about me. You have enough troubles of your own." Her eyes filled. "Again, I'm so sorry about your husband." She felt even guiltier for having suspected him. "If I had known what he was doing, I would have insisted he stop it right away."

What more could she do? She walked the older woman to her cottage and watched her pack. Then she waited with her until the taxi arrived.

Gazing after the vehicle's departing taillights, Caitlin slowly became engulfed by the surrounding darkness. Her mood also dark, she could imagine the night as a living, threatening entity. The moon had already slid into the blackness to the west. It must be two or three in the morning—no time to be out by herself.

Though there really was no safety if someone wanted you dead, she thought. Professor Abernathy had been killed earlier in the evening. Shivering again, remembering the way his poor, crumpled body had appeared in the headlight beams, she hurried into her cottage, locked the door and placed a chair beneath the knob.

Not that she was going to be able to sleep for more than two seconds.

Two seconds turned into two hours.

Caitlin was up and dressed at dawn. A heavy dew lay on the grass as she pointed the car toward Black Broch. Intent on finding Bain for that talk, she parked the car in a spot below the ruins, then climbed the hill. As on other occasions, the castle seemed deserted. Staring at the ragged window slits in the crumbling towers, she

wondered where and how on earth Bain hid his reno-
vated rooms.

She also shouted his name several times, only to hear
nothing but the lapping sound of the waves in the loch.

Then she tried something desperate—waving the falcon ring about, hoping it would change color. "I'm in
trouble, Bain! Come help me!"

The moonstone remained opaque and white, as if it
refused to give credence to her lie.

And no one answered.

"Damn!" She shouted one last time, "I didn't mean
you had to stay away forever!"

Silence. Lapping water. The flitting of a chill breeze
through her hair.

She sighed and pulled up the collar of her jacket.
Bain wasn't going to appear until he wanted to. If he
ever wanted to, after she'd told him off at the fair. Were
his feelings hurt? Even as she wondered, Caitlin knew
it was far more important to determine what part, if
any, Bain had played in Professor Abernathy's death.

She was tortured by the idea that someone had died
because of her, was even more tortured when she
thought of Bain killing the poor old man to protect her.

She couldn't believe it of the man she loved.

She wouldn't.

Only . . . she had to know for certain.

Wandering about the grounds of the castle for a bit
longer, she found a rough path that led along the edge
of the promontory. Sheer rock dropped to the loch,
more than fifty feet below, and boulders clustered at the
cliff's base. She peered over gingerly, able to understand how those women who'd jumped had met instant death.

Had those deaths been voluntary? Or had they, too, been murder?

Wandering further, Caitlin found a low doorway half overgrown with vines. The real entrance to Black Broch?

Excited, she scrambled in, only to gaze about an empty, musty chamber with an earthen floor. A huge length of chain hung on one wall. Was this all that remained of the castle's dungeon? Unfortunately, there were no other doors leading anywhere else.

She came out into the morning sunlight again and completely circled the ruins, looking for hidden doors, even exploring the shadowy courtyard. The torchlit rooms she'd seen haunted her. If she didn't know better, hadn't been inside the castle more than once, she would suspect that her imagination had run away with her.

She called Bain's name one last time before giving up and heading for her car.

If he heard her, he wasn't answering.

She wondered how she would live with herself until he did.

Lulled by the relative safety of sunlight, Caitlin slipped on her nightgown and slid into bed when she returned to the cottage, then found herself musing about the madwoman who'd been found in Black Broch's courtyard. She could understand how the woman had gotten to that unbalanced state, considering the crazy experiences she herself had had.

Caitlin wondered how she kept her own sanity. Perhaps she remained more centered because she blamed imagination for anything unusual. Creating art placed her in another reality of sorts. She could comfortably believe in all sorts of things at the imaginative level, yet keep her feet on the ground in the real world....

Sleeping deeply, she woke up with a start at dusk. Someone was pounding loudly on her door.

Caitlin sat straight up, staring into the room's deep shadows. "Who is it?"

"Mary MacDonald. Are you all right? We haven't seen you all day!"

She could hardly blame the woman for worrying, after the night before. She'd been remiss in not dropping by the manor house earlier. Rolling out of bed, she pulled on the kimono she used as a robe and opened the door to see Mary's concerned look.

"I was awake most of last night, so I've been sleeping all day."

"Thank heavens." Mary relaxed visibly. "We all had a bad night. You know, you can move into one of the bedrooms at the house if you like. You don't have to stay out here by yourself."

"Thank you. I'll think about that," she promised, knowing she wouldn't. If Bain ever showed, she'd be better off in the cottage.

"Meantime, would you like some supper brought to you? On the house, of course. You must be hungry."

"Food would be wonderful." She felt incredibly hollow.

Thanking Mary again before she closed the door, Caitlin switched on the lamp and stretched. Now she wasn't tired at all, would probably be awake another night.

But she didn't feel normally energetic. Deciding against getting dressed—she wouldn't have to change if she didn't go to the manor house—Caitlin retrieved her suitcases from the closet and started sorting through her clothing. She wondered if it wouldn't be best to book a flight home as soon as the police would allow her to leave the country.

The thought of leaving nearly broke her heart. She loved Bain Morghue, whoever he was, but it was no use trying to have a relationship with a phantom.

Knowing she could not leave, not until he told her to go, Caitlin set the suitcases aside.

Supper arrived, a big tray with thick soup, warm bread and fresh cheese. She ate more heartily than her appetite demanded.

Afterward, to keep her mind off Bain—the incessant questions and worries she had about him—she worked on her jewelry designs at the table beneath the cottage's main window. Her pencil flew as if possessed. New ideas flowed effortlessly. Soon she had covered at least a dozen pages with abstractions of the moon and darkness and swords with jeweled pommels.

Like Bain's claymore.

A bit ghoulish, but the designs were good. Perhaps she ought to create at night more often.

When she finally took a break, she glanced at her travel alarm. Five minutes after midnight.

Where was Bain now?

What was he doing?

Thinking of her?

"I need you, Bain Morghue," she whispered, twisting his ring on her finger. "God help me, but I do."

The wind had risen, and it soughed about the eaves. Longing to see the man she loved, Caitlin opened the curtains and leaned forward to catch sight of a sky full of silver stars, a westering moon, and low fog creeping over the ground. Soon the sky itself would be obliterated.

Then her breath caught as something stirred deep in the shadows. A huge form glided out of the blackness, towering, fluttering...

Frozen with fear, Caitlin clutched the windowsill until she realized she was looking at a big black horse.

The stallion stopped directly in front of the window, his nostrils blowing steam. On his back, Bain sat stone-still, his cloak flapping in the wind, his face harsh and stern. It was as if she had conjured him up, as she had when she was in trouble. Only this time, *he* was the danger.

For several seconds she stared, meeting him eye-to-eye, unable to suppress longings that were growing stronger by the minute.

Meetin' his eyes is a direct and true invitation.

Bridget's warning echoed through her head. Caitlin silently commanded Bain to take the damn invitation, and as he dismounted she flew to the door.

"Bain..." was all she managed to get out before he lifted her off her feet, kicking the door shut behind him.

He carried her to the bed, threw her down and moved over her in a flurry of heated flesh and cold clothing. He smelled like mist, moss, chilled salty wind. She cried out in her joy at seeing him. His eyes a fierce blue, he angled his head to ravish her mouth. Their tongues danced as he undid her kimono, then slipped it and her nightgown over her head.

Naked beneath him, she writhed when he sipped at her breasts with a warm, insistent mouth and parted her thighs to invade her secret, moist places. She arched and shuddered, nearly losing herself.

"I've missed you, lady," he muttered, the burr of his accent thicker than ever before. "Oh, how I've missed you."

Caitlin could only moan.

Bain rained kisses over her throat and shoulders as he opened her thighs wider to position himself between them. He took her hand and pressed it against his tumescence.

At the moment, Caitlin didn't care who he was or what he had done. She had never felt such passionate longing. "I want you," she whispered.

"Then have me."

Quickly unfastening his trousers, he lifted her hips and plunged forward to join them. She cried out, then wrapped her legs around his clothed legs. He thrust strong and fast, over and over, until the night itself seemed to pulsate. Caitlin arched her back and grasped his powerful shoulders.

He seemed intent on making them one. His heart and hers were beating a single rhythm together, and their limbs were so intertwined she didn't know where she ended and he began. Trembling, she abandoned herself to the inevitable, seeking a release. When it came, she cried out, the pleasure excruciating, the silver stars now burning behind her lids. Bain groaned and shuddered as he reached his own climax, then sank down atop her.

Some moments later, he rolled to the side and cradled her in his arms. Her cheek resting against him, Caitlin gradually realized he was still fully dressed. She unbuttoned his black shirt, running her hand through the light matting of dark hair on his chest. He helped her take the shirt off, then sat up to remove his trousers and boots.

As he did so, she remembered something other than the passion that had overtaken her. "Bain?"

"Yes, my heart." Naked, he lay down again and draped the bedclothes over them. "I was sorry I did not stop you as soon as you walked away."

She had to fight against the sensations he caused as he turned her toward him and caressed the length of her spine. She took a deep breath and tried to put some mental space between them. "I appreciate your apology, but...there's something else.... There's been a murder."

His expression changed. His gaze was steadier now, more alert. "Here?"

She nodded. "Professor Abernathy...the man I told you had been bothering me. He and his wife were staying in the next cottage." Noticing that Bain didn't react, she went on, "I mistakenly thought the professor was following me, meant me harm. But he was only worried about my welfare."

"As I suggested."

Though he still wasn't showing any emotion. "He was murdered, lying in a ditch all covered with blood! Don't you think that's terrible?"

"Aye. Murder is always terrible." He sighed and attempted to draw her closer.

But she held him off. "If it's so awful, how can you be so casual about it?"

"I have seen many awful things."

"But Professor Abernathy was innocent. He wasn't up to anything—he was a tourist, for heaven's sake. He didn't deserve to have his chest ripped open by a sword! There was blood all over—"

"You found the body?" he interjected.

She nodded and broke into a sob.

Murmuring softly, he drew her to him and kissed away the tears running down her cheeks. "Poor, sweet Caitlin, no wonder you are so distraught."

Her voice shook. "The police came and questioned everyone. We're all afraid some maniac is running around in the dark, looking for another victim." When she regained her composure, she asked, "Where have *you* been the past thirty-six hours?"

"Away."

"Away *where*?"

This time it was he who drew back to look at her. "Are you accusing me of this deed, lady?"

Her heart raced as she gazed deeply into his eyes. They held an open expression, not the sly expression of a murderer, of a man who could sneak up on another in the dark and leave him in a ditch.

"No," she finally said. That she truly did believe in his innocence seemed to lift a weight from her heart. "It's just that you do have a sword, and Professor Abernathy spotted someone skulking about my cottage. I thought he might have seen you."

Bain scowled fiercely, and she felt a serious thrill of fear. Then his gaze seemed far away, removed, as if he were focusing on something beyond her. "Aye, now I understand. 'Tis *his* doing."

"Whose doing?" she asked anxiously.

"My enemy. I should have expected this." Bain rose on his elbow to stare at the curtained window. "If he canna harm me or you, he will see that another suffers. He was always full of ruthless hatred."

"You know who killed Professor Abernathy?" She sat up, holding the sheet about her. "We have to tell the police!"

"'Tis not necessary. He shall meet his fate on his own. Even if he destroys me first."

Bain destroyed? She prayed he was exaggerating. "You can't let a murderer go free, or expect fate to take care of him. He's broken the law!"

"Broken many laws, Caitlin."

"What? When?"

His eyes glowed midnight blue in the lamplight. "I canna explain more."

"You're unbelievable!" she cried in frustration and outrage. "This is a murder we're dealing with here! If you won't go to the police, I will! Tell me the killer's name!"

"'Twould only place you in terrible danger."

"More danger than I'm in with a killer loose outside?"

He took her hand and touched the falcon on her middle finger. "The ring will protect you."

She ripped her hand from his. "I'm not in the mood for magic or visionary experiences." She'd seen death up close, real blood. "This is serious, Bain."

"Aye. Very serious." He sat up and, before she could react, scooped her up and slid her into his lap. "My heart would be fairly broken if anything happened to you."

Did that mean he loved her?

Bain stroked her hair and pressed kisses against her temple. The combination of romantic words—the kind she'd been longing for—and the proximity of his warm flesh nearly made her forget everything but him. Them. This moment. She slid an arm about his bare waist, appreciating the hard muscles of his back.

"I think of you when I am awake. I dream of you when I sleep," Bain murmured, lowering his head to take her mouth. "I am not nearly so alone since I found you at the crossroads, my brave Caitlin. There is some light in the darkness."

He spoke so intently, with such longing. Touched deeply, she stroked his cheek and pressed herself against him. The proof of his renewed desire throbbed against her hip.

He lifted her and turned her, then brought her down to straddle him. She didn't think to protest. She couldn't have resisted him even if she wanted to. . . .

This time they made love more leisurely, lips and hands touching, seeking. She closed her eyes, her hips undulating with his rhythm. Time had no meaning as they sought to become one again, her softness enclosing his hard strength. Bain stroked her breasts, her thighs, her belly, finally anchoring his hands at her waist. He lifted her and brought her down again, sliding her along his length. She moaned, and he moved faster, making their release as explosive and sweet as the last.

Afterward, Caitlin dozed in his arms, oblivious of danger or worries. When she stirred some time later, Bain lay on his back, perusing her history book, one arm cradling her against him.

"Where did you find that?" she asked sleepily.

"Between the bed and the wall."

"I must have been reading it in bed last night." Then, in spite of being groggy, she remembered the footnote. "Do you belong to the clan of MacBain?"

"I belong nowhere." He added, "Though I'm descended from the MacBains on one side of my family."

Trying not to react to his lonely statement about belonging nowhere, she continued. "Is the name Morghue Scottish?"

"'Tis closer to the ancient language.''

"Gaelic?"

"Aye, my mother's tongue."

Celtic. Morghue. The name wasn't so far from Mor-righan, if one really thought about it. In the soft, dark night, Caitlin could imagine Bain a haunted demon lover, the halfling son of the queen of the fairies. The Prince of Air and Darkness. But if she voiced such a theory, she would think herself crazy, even if he didn't.

So she continued with history. "Do you know about the feud within the MacBain clan? Are you descended from the misbegotten line?"

He turned to gaze at her closely. "I am not so cruel that I would bury a regiment of soldiers alive."

Or run a claymore through Professor Abernathy.

The thought came to her like a psychic flash. "But your enemy would—he's related to the misbegotten MacBains, isn't he?" And full of ruthless hatred.

Instead of answering, he kissed her. And she responded in kind. Even if she guessed the actual identity of the murderer, Bain probably wouldn't admit she was right. And he was in danger himself; he'd said so.

"I'm worried about you," she said. "This guy is trying to kill you, isn't he? Is Alistair MacDonald descended from the MacBains? Julian Taylor?" When he didn't answer, she grew exasperated. "You're so frustrating!"

"And here I thought I had taken care of your needs, lady." He turned her over on her back, moving over her.

"I didn't mean I was physically frustrated." Though he could get her to that state quickly, naked as they were.

He kissed her lips, her throat, her breasts, only pausing in his ministrations when he glanced at the window, now gray with dawn. "'Tis nearly day. I must go."

"Right away?" She couldn't hide her disappointment.

"I fear so." His movements reluctant, he rose to gather his clothing.

She didn't want to be clinging or possessive. She should be happy they'd spent so much of a night together. But she had to swallow a lump in her throat.

"You aren't leaving because I'm asking too many questions?"

"Nae, lady." He sat down on the bed to pull on his boots. "I have responsibilities."

Guarding ancestral lands or ruins from rival relatives? People could get crazy about that sort of thing, Caitlin knew. And it made as much sense as guarding the door to the invisible world.

"You don't sound very happy about your duties."

Bain leaned over to kiss her yet again. "I am sorely weary of them."

"Then why don't you quit? Surely you have a choice."

He mumbled a negative, nibbling her lower lip.

"You could change your life if you really wanted to," she insisted. "Why be miserable? For one thing, why don't you let the authorities deal with your crazed relatives?"

Which brought them back to the murder.

Ignoring her words, Bain got to his feet with a sigh. "I was happy this night, and that must do." Then he spotted her suitcases, and a couple of sweaters folded on a chair. "What is this? Have you been packing?"

"The murder had me scared silly. I was thinking about booking a flight home." Though she had given up on the idea for the moment.

Bain scowled at her. "You canna go. We are bound."

Telling her she *couldn't* go was different than begging her not to. He couldn't control her!

"You've said that before, but I'm waiting for proof." A shared interest in defying the darkness wasn't enough. "You've made no promises to keep me here."

"You must stay. You are nearly as caught as I myself."

Resentful, she sat up and defiantly pulled the sheet around her. "If I wanted to, I could get on a plane and be out of this country—and out of your life for good—before you could blink an eye."

He continued to scowl at her, but she refused to drop her gaze. Finally his expression changed. "Perhaps you *are* strong enough to break the tie." Fastening his cloak, he gave the suitcases one last glance, his expression remote now. "If you can leave, brave Caitlin, perhaps you should."

Then he opened the door and was gone.

Mouth open in shock, she sank back down against the pillows. First Bain had high-handedly told her she couldn't leave the country. Then he'd suggested she should.

How ambivalent. But then, perhaps he was so wrapped up in defending himself against his murderous relative, he didn't know his own mind.

How unfair. Despite what had gone on between them, Bain's final dismissal had been very cold. And, though he'd always come to her defense in threatening situations, she felt she'd been left to face fear and mayhem on her own.

CHAPTER ELEVEN

The next morning Caitlin groggily dressed herself. Not having gotten another wink of sleep, she now felt horribly out of sorts.

How dare Bain tell her to leave the country, especially after he'd claimed she was a light in his darkness, that his heart would break if anything happened to her! She had to face it: Bain Morghue was not only mysterious, but contradictory, as well.

But why? Because he was troubled? Or because he was in desperate straits of some sort?

Either way, she'd do well to get on a plane and fly back to California as soon as the authorities would allow it. Professor Abernathy's murder should be uppermost in her mind. She made a mental note to call Sergeant Cooke after breakfast to find out how the investigation was progressing.

Dressing to go to the manor house, she caught the falcon ring on the cardigan of her red sweater set. She gazed at the moonstone, thinking she ought to return such a priceless piece to its owner.

Damn it all, she'd *have* to see Bain again!

Thoroughly disgusted, she removed the ring from her finger and stuffed it into one of the cardigan's pockets. Bain had better not try anything funny when she turned his token over to him. She tended to lose her head whenever she was around him. She'd simply have to steel herself.

The morning sun was shining gloriously through the manor's windows when Caitlin joined Mary and Julian at the table in the dining room. Both of them were subdued, and Mary was sighing as she nibbled at a scone. A smile trembled about her lips when she saw Caitlin.

"I'm so happy you've come to breakfast. I hope your sleep wasn't too restless—I noticed the light was on all night."

"I caught a few winks." Caitlin wondered if her landlady had also seen Bain.

"I still think you should move into the manor house. I would feel much more at ease." Mary glanced at Julian. "I can understand masculine pride. But surely it isn't beneath a young woman to seek safety in numbers."

The Englishman took a sip of tea. "I'm simply more comfortable in my own little house. I would have to sort and repack to move out, even for a night." He clucked. "Such a lengthy and unpleasant task."

"I know how that is," agreed Caitlin, relaxing when she realized no one was going to mention any midnight sightings. The room was a bit too warm, so she slipped off her cardigan and hung it on the back of her chair. "Last night I went through my things. I hope I can stuff everything in my cases. I don't know how I always manage to bring back twice as much as I arrive with."

A solemn-faced Bridget entered the dining room, and Caitlin ordered orange juice and a poached egg for breakfast. A basket of scones and muffins sat in the center of the table, beside the tea pot.

"Have you been packing, Caitlin?" Julian asked.

"I took my suitcases out of the closet. That's a start, I guess."

"Oh, dear." Mary's mouth trembled again.

Which made Caitlin feel badly. "You have a lovely place...."

"I understand," the landlady interjected. "'Twould be best if you left, however." She sighed. "I'm only sad over this horrid situation, and I'm worried that other travelers won't be willing to come here."

"I'm sure it will all blow over," Caitlin assured her, "as soon as they catch the murderer and put him away." She only hoped, for Mary's sake, that one of her husband's swords wouldn't turn out to be the murder weapon. She glanced toward the door opening into the hallway. "Where is Alistair this morning?"

"Taking a walk."

"I could use a walk, too," remarked Julian.

Caitlin said nothing, hoping the Englishman wouldn't try to talk her into accompanying him. She no longer trusted either Julian or Alistair.

"I only hope the fresh air softens my husband's mood." Mary rolled her eyes. "He's so angry at the police, he wants to sell this house and move to another part of the country. And I'm so fond of the area. We used to stay here on holiday, even when we lived in Glasgow."

"Things will settle down," Caitlin said as Bridget delivered her orange juice and poached egg.

The housekeeper gestured to the basket of scones and muffins. "Ye should be eating, or ye'll be losing your strength."

"True." Caitlin reached for a scone.

Bridget frowned. "Ye've been losing weight."

"Only a few pounds." Her clothes *were* a bit loose now.

"Dinna fade away," intoned the housekeeper. "Not when there be a storm coming up the likes o' which we've nae before seen."

"Whatever are you talking about?" Mary asked, not trying to hide her annoyance.

"My sister was reading the tea leaves last night." Bridget's eyes grew round. "She saw the clash of mighty swords, the door to hell standing wide open, the face of the divil hisself!" Pausing to great effect, the housekeeper leaned closer to Caitlin. "'Twoulda been better if ye'd left long ago."

Chills shot up Caitlin's spine.

"Enough!" Mary demanded. "Please, we've had enough horror and fear in this house, Bridget. If you can't say something positive, say nothing at all."

As the housekeeper left, Caitlin thought to set her scone aside, since she was no longer hungry. But she *did* need her strength, she decided, so she forced herself to butter it and finish it, along with the egg and a cup of tea. Not that she wanted to believe the housekeeper's pronouncements.

A bit distracted—she had a lot to do—she rose from the table a few minutes later and took her leave of Julian and Mary. Headed for the door, she nearly ran into Alistair. He responded gruffly when she wished him good-morning.

Julian, on the other hand, cheerfully called, "Bon voyage, Caitlin, in case I don't see you again."

Alistair raised his brows. "She's leaving? Today?"

She had her hand on the doorknob. "More likely tomorrow or the day after."

Alistair grunted and turned away. Julian's smile fled.

And Caitlin left, unsettled, certain both men appeared disappointed that she wasn't leaving the country immediately.

Why?

Because they were concerned for her? Or because one of them—Bain's murderous enemy?—thought she was in the way?

After enjoying a solitary few minutes over a last cup of tea, he noticed Caitlin's red cardigan hanging on the back of a chair. Silly little American. He'd take it to her in hopes that he might speed her departure. She was definitely making the right choice in leaving Scotland. Picking up the sweater, he slung it over his arm. He was already out the door when he noticed a weight banging against his leg. He delved into the pocket, felt a round object and pulled it forth.

The falcon ring!

For a moment, hands trembling, he could only gape. Praise the ancient, evil gods!

For he held his enemy's personal token, and with it his enemy's life!

If he was quick enough, that is. And wise enough.

He murmured a few words in Gaelic to offset the spell on the moonstone before slipping it onto his little finger. He wanted no warning for Bain Morghue!

Then he threw the sweater aside and fairly sprinted for his quarters. He should take care of Caitlin, of course. The chit deserved to die, after all the trouble she'd caused. But he'd wait until later to slit her pretty throat. He had more important prey to stalk first.

When he reached his place of privacy, he bolted the door behind him and removed the long, narrow wooden box stuck between the bed's springs and mattress.

Thankfully, the police hadn't done a really thorough search, or they might have found it.

He could have handled them, of course, but policemen tended to be like ants. The more one stepped on, the more swarmed out of the hill. Besides, he would soon be beyond the reach of the law. With access to another world and power over its fierce denizens, he could come and go at will, could do exactly as he liked.

Opening the wooden box, he removed the precious dirk, along with the pencil portrait of Bain he'd stolen from Caitlin earlier. He held the deadly dagger up by the window, appreciating the way the light glittered on the gems sunk into its pommel, the way it glowed on the gold of its hilt. The blade was sharper and shinier than any earthly metal. He couldn't wait to draw blood with the weapon, to laugh in the face of his fallen enemy as he hefted the matching claymore and slung on the golden armor buried beneath Black Broch.

"Death to Bain Morghue!" he shouted to the rafters. He had fought the fiend before, but this time he would win!

Hardly able to contain himself, he changed to sturdier shoes and a warmer jacket before readying the dirk. Taking a length of narrow cord and the portrait, he folded the paper and tied it about the dagger's hilt.

"So much for your little harlot! Her repulsive, fawning love shall help kill you!"

Last but not least, he stood before the mirror on the opposite side of the room and raised the dirk.

"Hear me, O powers of evil!" he droned in Gaelic, holding the dirk high. "I am Atholl! Show me my enemy!"

He watched closely as the mirror clouded over, then cleared to reveal Black Broch on its promontory, waves dashing below. Heavy clouds broiled in the distance, and a tiny figure paced near the cliff.

Morghue!

"Cloak me, evil ones! Hide me from my enemy and his minions! Give me his life!" he demanded, his voice rising to a near shout.

For effect, he smashed the mirror, chortling as silvery shards flew through the air.

The time for waiting was ended!

Hiding the dirk beneath his jacket, he slammed out the door and ran to the car. There he flung himself to the ground to untie the antique claymore he'd secured beneath it, the weapon that had killed foolish Abernathy. He'd throw the inferior sword into the loch once he obtained the dirk's mate.

He placed the claymore in the back seat. Then he got into the car and spun its wheels, sending the vehicle shooting down the driveway.

"Death to the Prince of Air and Darkness!" he shouted. "By the hand of Atholl, the true heir of the MacBains!"

For in one fell swoop, he would gain unlimited power and gold, while finally avenging his ancestors!

In the shadow of Black Broch's main tower, Bain leaned against a battered wall and gazed down into the sea loch. Dark water splashed restlessly, sending spray flying up and over the rough faces of the bordering rocks.

A storm must be raging out at sea.

A storm that could be heading inland, Bain thought, observing the low-hanging gray clouds on the horizon. He cared naught. Let the cold rain fall, the ragged lightning split the sky, the tempestuous winds howl. The woman who had obsessed him night and day was leaving him behind.

Even now, if her strength hadn't deserted her, she could be winging her way back to her homeland . . . and safety. He had renounced his claim on her. He had bidden her goodbye. Only his dreams would be haunted by the lovely face, the soft, rounded body, the courageous warmth of spirit that had called out to him from the very beginning.

Brave Caitlin. Pure of heart. Sweet of soul, with a soaring vision. And even so, she was able to keep her feet firmly on the ground.

He had never met another of her like, had been tempted to tell her the whole truth, something he'd never before done. If anyone could accept him, help him face the life he'd grown deathly tired of, she was that woman. But because she was so special, because he cared so much, he'd had to let her go. He'd been truthful when he admitted that his heart would break if anything happened to her.

Unfortunately, in his world, *anything* could and did happen.

The clouds roiled closer. Bain stepped out onto the path that lay between the sheer drop and the ruins. A doorway to shelter lay behind him, but he wanted to feel the rain and the wind. He had walked several paces when his skin began to prickle. The tiny hairs on the back of his neck rose.

Danger?

Even as he stiffened, he realized that his enemy was close upon him. Far too close!

How had this happened? Where was the sentry?

With a crazy shriek, a dark figure suddenly leaped from the shadow of some fallen stones. The wild man was brandishing a sword in one hand, the stolen golden dirk in the other.

"Atholl!"

"What? Caught without your claymore, Prince?" The maniac snickered. "Isn't that too, too bad!"

Indeed, Bain's sword stood inside the doorway behind him. His enemy had managed to sneak up on him when he was unsuspecting and unarmed.

Bain shouted a curse.

"Spells won't save you now!" yelled Atholl, launching himself at the larger man.

Bain feinted, grabbing his enemy's sword arm. They both went down. Rolled. Struggled. Until, with a grunt, Atholl dropped the larger weapon.

But he still had the dirk that had once been Bain's own!

"Thief!" Bain snarled, wrestling with the man. Beneath Atholl, Bain reached up to grab his throat...and glimpsed the silver ring on his enemy's hand.

The token he'd given Caitlin!

Distracted, he loosened his grip.

And the dirk plunged downward, tearing a burning hole through his chest. Bain saw his own blood on the blade before Atholl slashed down a second time.

"Die, you monster!" his enemy howled.

Bain tried to rise, to throw off his attacker, but he was suddenly too weak. His muscles spasmed, and sharp pain radiated outward from the wounds.

Atholl pulled his arm back for another savage stab, his face a mask of hatred. Bain tried to hold him off, even though he was resigned to its being no use. Just then a wild flurry of feathers suddenly lunged from the sky.

The falcon!

With a scream of terror, Atholl dropped the dirk and rolled to the side, clutching his head.

"My faithful friend!" muttered Bain. Unable to rise, he focused all his psychic energy on his sentry.

The falcon swooped again and again, raking its claws along Atholl's back. Hands covering his wounded head in protection, his enemy crawled to the dirk and then on to the sword he had dropped. Bloodied and winded, he nevertheless staggered to his feet, weapons in hand.

"Gods protect you!" cried Bain to the bird as it descended, shrieking its war cry.

Atholl swung the sword and the dirk, missing with both. The falcon turned on the wind, talons extended and striking a swift and savage blow to the man's face. Rivers of blood spurted in every direction. Had the falcon taken an eye?

Bain could only watch from where he lay as Atholl screamed and ran, the sentry in pursuit. The horrible sound faded in the distance.

Bain dragged a hand to his chest. Warm blood seeped between his fingers; cold crept up from his legs. Gray clouds seemed to merge with the mist now flowing in with the current from the sea.

Was he dying?

Would he at last be free of his cursed life?

"Caitlin." Her name came no more than a ragged whisper from between his lips, which grew stiff with the effort. If only he could see her face again.

But was she safe, unharmed? How had Atholl obtained the moonstone ring?

Only for her sake did he cling to the solid earth beneath him, though he feared the effort would in the end be for naught.

"Caitlin!" he whispered, his voice weaker.

Then his eyes closed.

Caitlin had the most awful feeling.

She'd grown increasingly jumpy since returning to her cottage, so nervous she hadn't quite been able to decide what to do first—pack, contact Sergeant Cooke, or call the airlines. Since the cottages weren't equipped with phones, and she'd forgotten to ask to use the MacDonalds' at breakfast, she'd have to return to the manor house to make a call. So she'd attempted to put her artwork in order, only to be interrupted by someone loudly peeling out of the B and B's driveway, as if demons were nipping at his tires.

Had something happened?

She'd gone outside and looked around, spotting Bridget in one of the windows of the manor house, washing the glass panes. That seemed normal.

Next, she'd walked about the cottage complex, only to find each thatch-roofed whitewashed house quiet and deserted. Approaching Julian's place, she'd tried the locked door, then peered through the window. She hadn't been able to see very well, but nothing had seemed out of order.

Reassured, she'd returned to her own cottage and continued sorting and packing drawings.

But that had been an hour ago.

Now the uncomfortable feeling was back again, and she felt twice as uptight.

Physically and psychologically chilled, she hugged herself and started to put on her kimono. Then she realized she'd left her cardigan at the breakfast table . . . with the falcon ring in its pocket.

The missing token had to be the reason for her discomfort.

She hurried for the manor house, chiding herself for leaving such an expensive piece of jewelry lying about. It wasn't until she spotted the red sweater lying on the ground that she panicked. She knelt and felt the pocket, already knowing the ring would be gone.

Someone had stolen it.

Bain's enemy?

Could the thief use the ring for some sort of nefarious purpose? Grabbing the cardigan, she raced for the car and Black Broch!

Something told her that Bain was in danger!

CHAPTER TWELVE

Caitlin felt worse and worse as she sped toward the ruins. A huge weight pressed down on her, taking her breath away. A psychic warning? At some deep, inexplicable level, she believed that she and Bain were one, and she feared for his very life. He'd said his enemy wanted to destroy him.

He'd also said he was alone.

Perhaps she shouldn't care about that. He'd walked away from her without a backward glance. But she couldn't stand the thought of him being attacked or harmed and having no allies, no one to turn to.

Reaching the crossroads, she was forced to slow. A mist crept in from the sea, obscuring the road, blending with the low-hanging iron-gray clouds that hid Black Broch itself. Several fat raindrops fell on the windshield. Caitlin parked the car and struggled up the steep incline, her feet slipping on wet grass, the air about her cloying and electric, as if with suppressed lightning.

She shouted, "Bain!" as she neared the summit. Hearing no reply, she circled the castle, first in one direction, then the other. "Bain!" she called again, approaching the path that overlooked the loch.

Was that a sound? She stopped short, listening intently.

"Caitlin..."

Thick mist swirling about her ankles, she stepped forward carefully. "Bain? Keep talking! I'm trying to find you!"

She strained to hear an unintelligible mumble and a moan, then almost stumbled over him, lying before her. A dark stain spread across his chest. Falling to her knees, she realized it was blood.

"Oh, my God!"

He grasped her hand tightly. "Caitlin...you are not harmed."

The blood seeped from a ragged tear in his dark shirt. She forced herself to remain calm, to fight back hysteria. But his handsome features were so drawn, and his skin was so pale.

"We have to get you to a doctor!"

"Not necessary."

She couldn't hold back a sob. "I won't let you die!"

He smiled wanly. "Hold me."

"But you're hurt!" Carefully she slipped her arms about his shoulders, raising his head to her lap.

"Ah, that feels better."

Cradling him, she gingerly undid his shirt, expecting the worst. When she saw where the wound lay, she cried out. "I have to get you to a hospital!"

"'Tis not as bad as it looks."

Tears squeezed out of her eyes and ran down her cheeks. "Someone stabbed you through the heart!"

"Do not weep, lass. 'Tis not so deep." He wiped tears from her cheek with gentle fingers, then pulled his shirt open further. "See? The bleeding has almost stopped. The wound is painful, but not deadly."

Strangely enough, the wound didn't look so bad when she peered at the cut more carefully. "But your shirt... You've lost so much blood." She didn't understand....

"I am weak, but I will recover. I need rest, 'tis all. Take me to my bed."

"Bain!"

"Do as I ask. Please."

What choice did she have? She couldn't carry him off bodily. Sniffling, she rose, then helped him. He groaned and slung his right arm about her shoulders, leaning against her as she eased forward.

"How did this happen? Did your enemy attack you?"

His expression hardened. "Indeed. He lay in wait for me." His gaze accused. "He had the falcon ring."

She swallowed guiltily. "I—I took it off and left it in my sweater pocket. He must have found it." But who? Julian? Or Alistair? "You told me to leave.... I was planning to give the ring back to you."

"I am only thankful you are not harmed."

That touched her. "I'm only thankful that you survived."

"Sweet Caitlin." He brushed a soft kiss against her cheek.

They halted at the foot of a great tower, and Bain ran his hand along a crevice. A door swung inward.

"How on earth do you hide these secret doorways so well?" She was certain she'd exited on the other side of the ruins the first time she visited. "I searched for a way in the other day."

"If my doors could be found, they wouldna be secret."

He scooped up a sword propped against the wall inside. The sparkle of jewels and the sheen of gold were visible in spite of the dim light.

"Your claymore?"

"I couldna get to it before the man was upon me."

They descended a length of stone steps. A flaring torch hung in a sconce on the wall at the bottom.

He indicated the way to the left. "This way."

The passageway they entered was long and dark. Another torch flared at the end, and several heavy wooden doors opened on one side.

Bain stopped at the third. "My chamber."

Caitlin pushed the door open, revealing a spacious bedroom with a huge four-poster, a high shuttered window and a fireplace. A couple of claw-footed straight-backed chairs sat on a thick sheepskin rug laid before the cheerful blaze. She helped Bain recline on the plaid-covered bed.

"We need to clean your wound."

He motioned to a tall chest by the wall. A pitcher and basin sat on top. The water steamed as she poured it. Hot? How convenient . . . as if someone knew . . .

She brought the basin and a cloth to the bed. "This might hurt." Still worried, she hesitated. "If you're not feeling any better in an hour or so, if you're feverish, will you go to a doctor then?"

He laughed softly. "I *will* feel better."

She immersed the cloth and peeled back his shirt—it was stiff with drying blood—and nearly did a double take! "It's already scabbing over."

"Your love heals me."

Her love? She'd never told him how she felt. But when she was with Bain, thought and speech could meld, the impossible could seem probable, illusion could merge with reality . . . or was it the other way around?

Glancing at the shirt, with its ragged tear, she was reminded of her blouse, torn by a hound of hell. But she hadn't been dreaming when she found Bain today. She supposed the wound must have looked worse than it was because she'd been so upset. Maybe some of the blood had been the other man's.

She washed the cut, then helped him shrug out of the shirt. "You could use some antibiotics."

"A kiss will do."

"Are you trying to make jokes?" She had relaxed somewhat, now that she finally believed he wasn't at death's door. Actually, she was feeling a bit lightheaded. "What makes you think I love you, anyway?"

"You wouldna be here otherwise."

"Don't get too conceited. You can't be sure of that." She tried to ignore his closeness, his enticing masculine scent, remembering that she was ticked that he'd pushed her away the last time they were together. "You told me to get out of the country. I have a rule—I don't moon over men who don't want me around."

"I never said I didna want you, lady. I only said you *should* leave if you *could.*"

"Oh, meaning if I could find the strength to tear myself away from you? Right, we're supposed to be bound." She took the basin back to the chest and wrung out the rag to let it dry by the fire. "Though exactly what we're bound by, I'm not sure."

"You will find out . . . if you stay here long enough."

"Really? What's going to happen?" She couldn't help being sarcastic. "Are the fairies coming to carry me away?"

"'Tis not the outside threats that are the most dangerous," he said ominously.

Meaning that threats that came from the inside of a person were more frightening? Like delusions, withdrawal, suicidal depression?

She look at him closely. "I agree that fear itself is the greatest enemy, any sort of negative emotion." Her brother's fear had cut him off from the outside world; Neil Howard's had made him paranoid. She approached the bed. "You need a bandage."

"Use another cloth."

She fetched it and came back. "Speaking of outside threats, this enemy of yours didn't do a very good job today. He jumps you, leaves a flesh wound and runs away?"

"Only because the falcon dived from the sky and attacked."

"Did it rake him with its talons?" She shivered, thinking of the time the falcon had dive-bombed her.

"My enemy was hurt sorely. I owe the bird my life." He glanced up at the window. "Could you open the shutters, so that he may come in when he wishes? I saw him last chasing after Atholl."

"Atholl? Is that the name of your enemy?" The window being high and sunk into the deep wall, she had to take a poker from the fireplace to reach the shutters. They opened, revealing pale, swirling mist outside. "I don't know any Atholl." And she'd been wrong to suspect either Alistair or Julian. "You needn't have tried to hide his identity."

"Merely mentioning the name could have placed you in danger. He is a madman who toys with black magic. He is desperate to slay me, and would threaten anyone who stood in the way."

She recalled that Bain had said his enemy was full of ruthless hatred. The man had certainly been hateful in murdering Professor Abernathy.

"He wants my inheritance," Bain continued, his eyes glittering.

"You mean Black Broch?" She sat on the edge of the bed.

"Aye, and my weapons, as well. Already he possesses the dirk that matches my claymore. He stole it from me some years ago."

"Because he thinks he's the true heir of the Mac-Bains, right?"

"And that the weapons will make him invincible."

"They're magical?" She stared at the sword, almost able to understand. It looked like something from a legend. But magical tales were one thing, assault and murder another. "I still think you should report this Atholl to the police. He can't go around attacking and killing people."

"He shall meet his fate."

Fate again! But she'd have to accept Bain's decision to avoid the police for the moment.

Bain yawned.

"I suppose I should let you rest."

"Perhaps 'twould be best. I am very tired, and may have work to do later. Could you pull off my boots?"

She tugged off the tall boots and dropped them on the floor, then helped take off his trousers. He wore nothing beneath, and was gorgeous from head to toe. She took a deep breath.

"I can be at your disposal later, as well, lass." He sounded smug. And infinitely seductive.

Flushing, she flipped a cover over him. "So you're going to take a nap?"

"You are welcome to sleep beside me."

To distract herself, she asked, "Any food around here?"

"The kitchen." He waved toward the door. "Turn right. At the end of the hall, go down another flight of stairs. You'll pass three doors. The fourth is the kitchen."

Three doors? More stairs? How big was Black Broch, anyway?

"Keep track of where you are. Do not be wandering about," Bain warned her, sounding sleepy. "You could become lost."

How did he hide all the rooms and passageways? She started to ask, but saw that he had nodded off.

Folding his trousers and placing them on one of the chair seats, she almost knocked over a slim easel she hadn't noticed in the flickering firelight. A portrait of a woman sat upon it, and, surprised, she recognized herself. Bain had kept the portrait from the fair.

How sweet.

Gratified . . . no, thrilled . . . she smiled. Before leaving the room, she took one last look at him. His dark lashes feathered strong cheekbones. The mouth that could be so hard looked soft and sensuous. Moved to kiss him, she held back, fearing he'd awaken. His wound might be minor, but it had apparently exhausted him.

Opening the door, she entered the dim passageway. Spooky. But she shouldn't be frightened. Surely Atholl, the madman, couldn't get in, since the doors to the outside world were hidden. Might she run into anyone else? Ghillie? She supposed she should have asked Bain where his servant was.

Her footsteps echoed off the stone walls. She jumped when a torch hissed as she passed beneath it. She really wasn't certain where she was going. But then, she hadn't known where she was going with Bain from the very beginning. She'd simply had to trust.

He drove some distance to a hospital in Inveraray, not wanting anyone in Droon to suspect what had been going on. He'd nearly fainted from the hot pain the razor-sharp talons had inflicted. Blood caked the left side of his face and ran from his many wounds. His lid had been slit, but his eye was intact, thank the gods.

The staff on emergency duty had *ooh*ed and *aah*ed. He'd received dozens of stitches while telling them some drivel about coming upon a falcon's nest on the cliffs by the sea. They'd wanted to keep him overnight, but he'd refused.

He couldn't afford to delay the second step of his plan.

The guardian of Black Broch was dead—at least he prayed so—but he needed to cast strong, dark spells to complete his work. The hours near midnight were best for that, though, weakened as he was, he would have to rest and wait until the next night.

He curled his lip as he thought about wringing the nasty little falcon's neck. A creature of day, it should be easy enough to catch after dark. Unless the bird could take other forms. He made a mental note to be on guard.

Meanwhile, sore and slightly woozy, he bought himself some new clothing, changed and paid for a room at a small hotel. Then he took a pain pill and lay down on the bed to peruse the aged leather-bound book.

The invisible world.

The door no mortal man had ever opened...and lived to tell the tale.

Until now.

Following Bain's directions, Caitlin located the kitchen. Like the rest of the castle, it had no electricity and seemed deserted. But someone had cooked the pot of stew bubbling in a modern-looking pot hanging in the huge fireplace. And someone had also set a round of cheese next to the fresh-baked bread on the room's wooden central table. Furtively looking around to make certain she was not being watched, Caitlin helped herself, then cut more bread and cheese to wrap in a towel and take upstairs.

She brought along a thick tallow candle in its holder. The windows of Black Broch were high, narrow and shuttered, the torches burning on the walls few in number. She needed any extra light she could find.

But even with a candle to guide her, she swore the return trip took much longer. Bain had said there were three doors to pass between the stairs and the kitchen, but Caitlin counted four. Was she lost?

She paused, noticing that the nearest doorway gaped open. Curious, she peered inside. The light from the candle glinted off rows and rows of books. A library? Though the room was narrow, its ceiling soared and wooden shelves climbed to the very top. Fascinated, she inhaled the musty odor of aging paper and leather and went inside. She held the candle aloft—Dickens, Shakespeare, Robert Burns and other classics nestled between volumes of history and books in all sorts of foreign tongues. There even seemed to be a couple of scrolls lying on a shelf high above.

What a collection! Alistair MacDonald would kill for the chance to examine it. Alistair... Atholl? Could they be one and the same? Had that scholarly man tried to kill for Bain's inheritance? Caitlin wondered.

One large book had handwritten letters on its spine— *The Demon Lover.* Instantly intrigued, she pulled it out and opened the yellowed pages, thoroughly fascinated when she recognized it as an old sketchbook. And what exquisite illustrations it held, watercolor combined with pen-and-ink, all bordered with swirling Celtic designs, and each accompanied by text in calligraphy.

Caitlin placed the candle nearby and sat down on the floor, carefully turning the fragile pages back to the beginning. The first drawing portrayed a beautiful woman with long black hair and a deep red gown— The Queen of Air and Darkness. The text related the same tale she'd heard from Alistair, how the sometimes cruel and capricious queen fell in love with a mortal and stole him away. Except in this version, the mortal was named—a legendary Scottish chieftain, the MacBain.

MacBain? Caitlin's eyes widened.

The MacBain loved his queen, but missed his warrior companions and his world. The fairy queen allowed him to magically appear on battlefields to help his allies. Still, weakened by a terrible blood feud, the chieftain's clan eventually fell into disarray and was taken over by its enemies, the descendants of the MacBain's evil, misbegotten half brother.

Caitlin felt chills. Awed by art that took her breath away—battles, ancient ships on tossing seas, tender scenes of the queen and her lover in forest glades, fairy rades rendered in fabulous detail—she read and reread the text, letting it sink in. She specifically focused on the part about the couple's son. Half mortal and half fairy, he belonged to neither world, and guarded the door that connected the two.

Now, reading the legend again, with a MacBain playing the part of the stolen mortal lover, she couldn't help but see Bain Morghue in the role of the son and guardian. It might only be a fairy tale, but it seemed eerily appropriate. And hadn't Bain said his father was some sort of warrior or soldier of fortune?

Anxious to get to the end of the tale, she turned another page and swallowed her disappointment when she found it blank. The pages that followed were, as well, though smaller pencil sketches had been stuck between them. Sighing, she examined several sketches closely. The beauty of the work was such that she was certain the same artist had created them.

One in particular attracted her, a study for a medallion, an abstraction of two figures who faced one another, legs and arms intertwined. The design was lovely, though the faces weren't finished. Caitlin wondered why. Anyone could see that one of the figures should be female, the other male. The Celts thought male and female to be a magically balanced combination, and it was the inspiration for many of their motifs, including the famous even-armed cross.

Knowing she shouldn't, but tempted to show Bain anyway, she removed the postcard-size drawing of the medallion and carefully placed it in the pocket of her cardigan. Then she rose to put the sketchbook back on the shelves. Another loose piece of paper drifted down to the floor. She stooped to pick up the drawing, a heroic study of a man on horseback. Frowning, she held it closer to the candle to get a better look.

It took her only a moment to recognize the handsome, cloaked rider on the black horse: Bain Morghue.

Some other artist had drawn him... and left her mark at the bottom of the page. Caitlin's mouth dropped as she noted the drawing's title, the artist's signature and the date: *The Prince of Air and Darkness, Janet Drummond, 1902!*

Something snapped inside Caitlin. Since the murder, her days and nights had been reversed. Maybe her confused inner time clock had something to do with it—maybe her horror when she'd thought Bain mortally wounded—but she fully believed Janet Drummond's drawings. On the way upstairs, she gazed about, certain she was traversing an enchanted castle with rooms that were never-ending and ever-changing, with doors that magically appeared and disappeared.

Was she doomed to disappear herself, she wondered, never to be seen again, like Janet Drummond? What or who lurked in the shifting shadows of the endless passageways? Or would madness take her to the promontory and death?

Not if she could help it!

She burst into Bain's bedroom. Wearing only a plaid, he stopped stroking the falcon, which was perched on the back of a chair, and gave her a startled look. The falcon shrilled and flew up to the window ledge.

Caitlin brandished the paper in her hand. "You've got some explaining to do! Look at this!" She pushed the drawing of the horseman under his nose.

He raised a brow. "Very nicely done."

"I'm not asking you for a critique." She had no patience for his clever evasions now. "Look at the signature and the date."

"Where did you get this?"

"From your library, where I found a sketchbook of Janet Drummond's drawings." When he continued to appear uncomprehending, her temper surged. "I should have known you'd play dumb about this!"

"Dumb about what, lady?" He took hold of her shoulders. "Sit down, now. You are all aflutter."

She shook him off, ignoring the expanse of muscular body exposed by the casually draped plaid. "I don't want to sit. I want some answers! Do you...did you know Janet Drummond? Did you pose for this portrait?"

He glanced at the drawing. "1902. Do I look as if I were more than a hundred years old?"

Of course, he knew that wouldn't seem possible. "But this *is* you."

"You think it bears a resemblance?" He stepped closer to peer intently. "Perhaps a wee bit, especially about that long, ugly nose..."

"No sarcasm, please! I'm not in the mood. What is Janet Drummond's work doing in your library?"

"My family's library," he told her. "A collection that spans centuries."

"She was one of the women who disappeared, maybe died, in the vicinity of Black Broch," she rushed on breathlessly. "Alistair MacDonald said several were pushed off the promontory, and one was found raving mad in the courtyard."

"Perhaps the man was trying to frighten you."

She sighed at the glib answer. What had she expected? "So you deny knowing anything about Janet Drummond, or that women have died here?"

"I didna say I knew nothing of a woman named Janet Drummond. And many people have died on this land over the centuries."

"Please, I don't want to hear about the buried soldiers again. Let's get back to Janet."

"And so we shall," he agreed. "If you'll only sit down and catch your breath."

Making a sound of exasperation, she took a seat on one of the claw-footed chairs before the fireplace.

Bain reclined across from her and gazed into the leaping flames. "Janet Drummond was a local artist whose work was inspired by other worlds. She became lost in it, obsessed by beauty she herself could not possess."

"But what happened to her? She walked away from her home, and no one ever saw her again."

"Where do people go when they waste away?" He shrugged. "I believe Janet was the lady who was found raving in Black Broch's courtyard."

"In 1931? The woman in the courtyard was young. Janet would have been well into middle age by then. And even if she was the one found in the courtyard, where had she been for nearly thirty years?"

He looked impatient. "I have tried my best to answer you, Caitlin. I canna do more." And he reached across to touch her.

She pulled back. "I don't think so."

He frowned. "What is wrong?"

"Something's very much awry. Things don't make sense."

"You are tired. Come and lie down...."

"I don't want to lie down. And I've had it with moonstones that turn blue, and magical swords, and wounds that heal on their own." She stared at the scabbing, which seemed somehow less thick than before. "I've had it with secret doors and rooms that can't possibly exist." She jumped up and glanced about. "How can this chamber and the vast hallways out there fit into the space of Black Broch's ruins, massive as they are?"

"You are distraught...."

"More than distraught. I'm tired of making excuses for things that I've seen with my own eyes. I admit I have a good imagination, but I couldn't dream up all this in a million years." She looked him boldly in the eye. "Janet Drummond was illustrating a story called *The Demon Lover*, about the fairy queen and a Mac-Bain. She drew you as their halfling son, the Prince of Air and Darkness." She held up the horseman sketch for effect. "And *are* you?"

The smile flickering about his lips held no warmth.

She repeated, "Are you the Prince of Air and Darkness?"

He suddenly rose, all smooth muscle, and approached to tower over her. "What if I were?"

The threatening pose surprised Caitlin, prompting her to drop the drawing.

"You would be in trouble, wouldn't you?" he asked, his voice all soft threat.

Taking hold of her shoulders, he lifted her right off the floor and anchored her against the wall. He was so strong, she felt a thrill of fear. His eyes burned deep and blue, his hot breath fanned her face.

"You want me to be a demon lover, don't you, Caitlin? A man who lures you into his world of darkness and keeps you in his thrall. Shall I take you to my bed, ravish you till you forget the daylight, till you know nothing but my name?"

He gave her no chance to answer, crushing her to him and covering her mouth with a punishing kiss. In spite of the situation, she felt herself responding.

At first.

But she wouldn't be manhandled. And she *would* handle her fear. "Stop it!" she cried, squirming. "Stop it, Bain. I don't want you this way!"

He lifted his head, breathing hard, his expression still angry. He released her, and she fell back against the wall, shaky.

"You should be knowing your heart, lady. One minute you are weeping because I am wounded. The next you are badgering me with furious questions. You have more than once accused me of murder. You must take me as I am, or not at all."

She conceded, "I don't think you're a murderer."

"Even when I told you to leave, I did so for your own good. I have always tried to protect you."

She had to admit the last was true—he'd come to her rescue at least four times—but she asked, "Protect me from *what?*"

"My life, lady. My enemies. My obligations. Sharing my existence is not for the faint of heart."

"Sharing your existence? We've only been on one actual date and spent half a night together."

His eyes were haunted. "I canna ask you for more, Caitlin, no matter how I love you."

"You love me?"

"With all my heart and soul."

He'd never admitted such before!

"But 'tis too much to ask you to risk everything for me."

"You make it sound like you're doomed or something. Please—I want to understand."

"Nae, 'tis impossible. I canna violate my oath...."

He had sworn not to tell? "Much of what I've heard and seen seems like a dream. And sometimes my imagination is overactive." She gestured toward the drawing lying on the floor. "But I didn't create this picture asleep or awake. I deserve explanations. And I don't deserve to be pushed off the promontory."

"The women who died there were not murdered."

"Suicide?"

"More like a loss of wits. But you need have no fear the same will happen to you, Caitlin, for you are braver than the danger inside. You are not tortured by guilt or anger or even fear. You have no need to run from your life."

"What was Janet Drummond running from?"

"Greed. She married an old man for his money."

"And the others?"

"The desire to escape responsibilities, to titillate their senses, to gain some sort of power..." He shrugged. "The pure of heart will always survive."

Realizing he meant her, she stepped closer. "I'm not perfect. And I'm certainly not selfless."

"As close as a mortal can be," he insisted. "You fought the darkness for your brother. You tried to help a man who carried demons on his back. You create art because you want beauty for a world that is often ugly." He touched her face, his expression softening. "And you want magic to be real, because you think it could make the savage world a better place."

True, she'd always been drawn to magical art and its fantasy realms. She believed crystals and spells and such could overcome all obstacles and impossibilities.

Embarrassed, she demurred, "You make me sound like a Goody Two-Shoes."

His gaze was intense. "Nae. The woman I love."

"Oh, Bain." She went to him, wrapped her arms about his neck. "I love you, too. Our love is an even more important reason for honesty. I don't know where to find you—"

"I have always found you when you needed me."

He kissed her deeply, pressed her close, winding part of the plaid about her. Before she was too distracted, she pressed a finger lightly against his lips.

"One more thing."

He smiled. "And what is that, my heart?"

"When you love someone, you're concerned for him, Bain. You want to know his enemies. You want to help." Even as she spoke, his smile faded and his expression darkened. "And don't give me some tripe about being doomed or cursed. If you are the Prince of Air and Darkness—" She was startled to realize that their conversation had proceeded as if that premise were true "—then there must be a way to change your circumstances. Even a spell can be broken. How does one free the Guardian of the invisible world?"

Again, Bain was stunned at the depth of Caitlin's caring. No other woman had ever made such an inquiry.

"I canna ask you for that, lady."

"Yes, you can." She seemed to know instinctively that she was the key.

"I willna ask you for it." For this went beyond danger.

"Ask."

He sighed, as usual, feeling compelled when she was so intense and heart-serious. "You would have to travel through the grave, into death itself."

Her eyes widened. Then she shivered. And he knew she was afraid.

He tightened his hold on her and stroked her back. "Nae think of anything but this moment, lady."

Quickly, passionately, he kissed her lips, her throat, then stooped to lift her off her feet and carry her to the bed. He made love to her as if it were their last hour on earth. He branded her with his mouth, invaded her with his tongue, strove to become one with her soft, quivering body. He wanted her to be the woman he had always waited for. The lover he had come to believe did not really exist.

But even so, he realized that was next to impossible.

She would need time to believe the truth she felt but could not accept.

And more time to learn to appreciate her true strength.

Time.

Something else his enemy had stolen from him.

CHAPTER THIRTEEN

Blue sky and sunlight. Though the sight was only a sliver through the open shutters of the chamber's high window, Caitlin felt wonderful.

Bain loved her!

She stretched in the great four-poster, then yawned. The fire had died down, but her man lay against her, offsetting any chill from the broch's stone walls. She touched the dark hair spilling over his forehead, making sure he was real, flesh and blood.

He murmured contentedly in his sleep.

Her memories of the night before, their conversation about the Prince of Air and Darkness, seemed like a dream. She had been so tired and upset, had been through so much, she understood how she could have slid into a skewed state of mind.

But had her mind really been askew?

She'd believed in magic and mythical guardians implicitly at the time. And Bain had seemed to go along with her.

"Good morning to you, sweet Caitlin," he said suddenly, startling her and anchoring her in the present.

"You're awake." She turned and slipped an arm about his neck, meeting the deep blue of his eyes. "Good morning."

He kissed her, then squinted at the window. "Though 'tis more like afternoon than morning."

"We slept all day?"

"More or less. Are you as hungry as I? There will be food in the kitchen."

"I could eat a shipload of bread and a side of beef." Judging from the rumblings of her stomach, they *had* slept a long time.

Bain swung his legs over the side of the bed and started to dress. Caitlin rose more slowly and searched for her clothing. The shell of her red sweater set lay on the floor on one side of the bed, and the cardigan on the other, along with her pants. Bain had to help her find her socks and shoes, thrown to the room's corners.

"You were very enthusiastic last night," she said teasingly.

"Aye." He seared her with his glance. "And I will be very enthusiastic again, once I fill my belly."

She assumed a sexy pose. "Really? Hope you're planning on wearing your plaid. It can get a woman going."

He growled and made a grab for her, but she ran away, laughing, enticing him into following her out the door.

"There's nothing like a man in a skirt."

"'Tis not a skirt," he objected.

"'Tis, too!"

Even the torches seemed to burn brighter as they headed for the kitchen, their laughter bouncing off the walls. A veritable feast was waiting on the kitchen's wooden table—a decanter of wine, a huge fresh salad, hot bread and cookies, a bowl of ripe strawberries, several succulent cheeses and, in the fireplace, a huge roasted turkey.

Caitlin piled her plate high and dug in. Her appetite had returned full-force. "Mm-hmm... Who's the cook—Ghillie?"

Busy chewing, Bain nodded.

She hadn't seen the strange man with the tufted ears since the day she and Bain had met. "Where is he, anyway?"

He wiped his mouth. "Who knows? He comes and goes. You can always find him in the kitchen in the mornings, if you are of a mind to."

"Is he your servant or not?"

"He helps with the household duties."

"A good little brownie, hmm?"

Bain merely smiled, while Caitlin continued musing about brownies—household fairies who were very shy and rather homely, but wonderful cooks and housekeepers. She glanced at the kitchen's stone floor, which had been swept and scrubbed clean enough to eat on. But she'd be darned if she was going to ask any more questions about legends or mythical people.

She and Bain were having such a nice time that she was reminded of the fair. Avoiding the darker events that had come afterward, she mentioned how much she had enjoyed herself that evening, and learned that Bain had attended all kinds of fairs in various parts of the British Isles. They discussed games of chance and carnival rides, as well as knightly tournaments and theatrical performances.

"So you've seen almost every play of Shakespeare's performed in the open air?" she asked, sipping at her wine.

"Aye. Though my favorites are the comedies, such as *A Midsummer Night's Dream*." He chuckled. "Once

I saw a tragedy become a comedy—when a flock of sheep came running across the stage in *MacBeth* instead of armed men.''

''Now, if the sheep had been wearing swords, that would have been even funnier,'' said Caitlin, giggling.

They both laughed. She wished they could always be this relaxed. No doubt being in a castle, removed from the outside world, helped. But she would soon have to face that world, and the sometimes frightening events that connected her with Bain. She glanced toward the kitchen's shuttered window, unable to see so much as a crack of light.

'''Tis already dark on this side of the broch,'' said Bain. ''The sun is sinking.''

''Already? My sense of time is all turned around.''

Unable to walk away from a meal without trying to clean up, she scraped any remaining food into a bowl and wiped off the table with one of the cloth napkins. Then she noticed that Bain was sitting stiffly, a scowl upon his face. The change in mood was like night and day.

Her throat tightened. ''Is something wrong?''

He stared at the window. ''I thought I heard the falcon's call.'' He rose. ''I will open the shutters.''

Now Caitlin could hear the shrill whistle, as well. She ducked when the bird fluttered through the window a moment later and landed on the fireplace mantel. Its beak was half-open, its bold eyes were glittering, and its wings beat the air frantically.

''Something *is* wrong,'' muttered Bain.

''What?'' Her heart sped up. So much for their peaceful interlude.

Bain motioned for her to accompany him out of the room. "Come."

"Your enemy?" she asked, the wind suddenly gone out of her. "I thought he was badly hurt."

"Not badly enough. I must prepare."

He strode purposefully down the passageway and she had a hard time keeping up. "Where are we going?"

"Outside."

"Wouldn't it be safer in here?"

"Not for you," he muttered as they went up the stairs and down another passageway, a different corridor from the one onto which his bedchamber opened. Slanting upward, it was more like a ramp.

Caitlin couldn't understand why she'd be safer outside—she'd just been thinking about how secure the castle felt. She started to object when they stopped and a big door swung open, flooding the passageway with moist, cool air and the dim light of the gloaming hour.

Bain took her in his arms and kissed her. "Go. Leave this place before 'tis completely dark. Atholl comes."

"Leave you?" She clung to him instead of letting go. "You were stabbed the last time this Atholl came visiting! I'm not going anywhere!"

"You must go, my heart." He kissed her again, his mouth softer, more lingering, his expression somber and frightening. "And if I dinna see you again, remember my love."

She panicked. "What are you talking about? What do you mean, I might not see you again—"

He cut her off with "I have my duties."

Which made her furious. "Your duties as Guardian?" Because of which his very life was in danger! "So we're back to that. What about that traveling-through-the-grave-into-death-itself stuff?''

"I told you, I canna ask you for that." He pushed her away. "And you are not ready. Our time has been too short. Keep yourself safe, sweet Caitlin."

"Bain!" she cried, ready to commit to anything to remain at his side.

But even as she spoke, the door slammed shut.

"Bain!" She pounded on the solid rock. "Damn!" Her hands hurt! And she was locked out again!

Unbelievable! Weeping with frustration and anger that she couldn't control her emotions, she slumped to the ground. How had she imagined that everything could ever be all right between her and Bain Morghue? He might be the most fascinating man she'd ever known, the most passionate, but he was also the most impossible and elusive—and his life-style was certainly the most bizarre of any man she had ever known.

She pulled herself together as the gray of gloaming turned to the gloom of oncoming night. And though the moon rose in the east, a great mass of clouds approached from the west, threatening to shut out any promise of light.

Still, Caitlin refused to slink off. If nothing else, if she was very quiet, she reasoned, she might somehow catch sight of this Atholl and identify Professor Abernathy's murderer to the police. Crouching behind a massive fallen stone, she felt her pockets, relieved that she still had her car keys. As soon as Atholl arrived, she could run for the vehicle, which was parked at the bottom of the hill, and drive to Droon to fetch Sergeant Cooke. Surely he and his crew could stop any serious violence.

The clouds roiled closer. Heavy waves splashed in the loch. The darkness deepened and thickened with mist from the sea. In the distance thunder rumbled, and Caitlin shivered with cold, though her resolve remained unchanged. She pulled her cardigan about her more tightly, and her hands froze in position when she thought she heard a skittering sound.

A pebble disturbed by a passing foot?

Listening carefully, she hardly dared breathe. When she heard nothing else, she slowly rose to a standing position. But she could see little in the dim moonlight. Only the outline of the broch's walls seemed blacker than the night.

She shivered again and started to sink back behind the stone. Then she was jerked up again, so hard that her teeth clacked together. A hand clutched her arm like a vise.

"Well, what have we here?" asked a silky, nasty, familiar voice. "If it isn't the prince's little harlot."

"Julian! You're hurting me!"

"Good!" He jerked her again, as if to show his authority. "I shall do far more before this night is over!" He laughed crazily. "Your suitor is dead! Did you find his body, or have you merely been pining away, waiting him for him to appear?"

He thought he'd killed Bain! Upset and in pain, Caitlin nevertheless made note of that. Then she cried out when Julian slapped her face. "Ah!"

"I am your master now. You will show me respect!" he snarled, his voice rising. "Answer me when I speak to you!"

Stunned, she struggled to think. "Uh, I—I'm mourning the prince. I found him."

Julian cackled and half pushed, half dragged her toward the nearest standing wall. Fearful, she decided she would try her best to go along with the madman. Bain had said he was preparing and would surely appear. She didn't want Julian forewarned.

Muttering in Gaelic, he touched the edge of a stone, and a door gaped open. Light pooled from the passageway.

She caught her breath in surprise. "You know how to get into this place?"

"I am Atholl, the great adept! My powers are mighty and endless!"

He was truly, deeply insane!

And terribly disfigured, she realized as soon as she caught sight of his face. One eyelid was swollen to twice its size, while red, painful-looking welts ran down both sides of his face. The falcon had wounded him sorely all right—the cuts were crisscrossed by numerous stitches. No longer sleek, his hair stood up in tufts where the welts ripped into it. Both eyes were bloodshot.

She tried to mask her horrified look too late.

He curled his lip. "So you think I'm ugly?" He shook her yet again. "Well, perhaps I shall sweeten the evening with some light diversion."

He wore a claymore on a belt outside his coat. From inside the garment, he drew forth a long knife with a sparkling, twining gold handle—the dirk that matched Bain's claymore. Smiling, licking his lips, he showed the dagger to Caitlin.

"Tonight I shall enjoy the dual pleasures of taking your body and slitting your pretty throat."

"Y-you're going to kill me?" And rape her? Dear Lord, where was Bain?

Julian started down the passageway, pulling her along. "The question is, do I want to kill you before or after I open the door to the invisible world?"

So that was what he thought he was about. Hoping she could buy some time by playing along with him, she suggested, "Why don't you throw me to the unseelies? Some goblins, maybe? Wouldn't that be more fun?"

"No, no, I want to do it myself!"

Again Caitlin prayed for Bain to come to her rescue. As strong and as crazed as Julian was, she feared she wouldn't be able to get away from him on her own. They came to a flight of steps and descended, entering another nightmare passageway. She only wished she were dreaming! He pulled her faster, and then quickly came upon more stairs, these twisting and winding deep into the castle.

"Where are we going?"

"To the lowest basement, my dear." Continuing downward, they passed a torch, and Julian glanced nervously up at the rafters high overhead. "You haven't seen a falcon about this evening, have you?" He sneered. "I have a taste for roasted fowl."

Without thinking, she blurted out, "The only roasted fowl I've seen around here was a turkey."

"Turkey?" He stopped short, nearly causing her to stumble. "You dare to make fun of Atholl?" His eyes blazed. "Cheeky harlot!" He smacked her across the face so hard, she saw stars. "I should slit your throat this very minute! You were too good to have dinner with me, eh? Too busy wasting away for your pretty prince!"

The coppery taste in her mouth was blood. He'd split her lip. And charged her adrenaline!

"Bain has ten times your courage! He didn't attack a poor old professor and run a sword through him!"

She realized too late that she'd spoken as if Bain were still alive. But Julian didn't react.

"Professor Abernathy," he mused. "Yes, that was a nice piece of work. Too bad you couldn't have seen it." He started down the stairs again, pulling her behind him. "Even worse that you couldn't have seen the way I dispatched your prince. Incidentally, I appreciated the ring you left in your pocket. It was very helpful."

Caitlin remained furious enough to goad him. "Why slit my throat? Why not bury me alive like those soldiers your ancestor killed?"

"Wonderful idea, but not quite personal enough."

"Your ancestor was an evil pig, and so are you! You shame the MacBains!"

He merely chortled and dragged her out of the stairwell into a long room with an earthen floor. A huge chain dangled against one wall among great tapestries hung on long poles and between standing suits of armor. It took Caitlin a moment to recognize the crumbling dungeon she'd stumbled across a day or so ago. Though the room had obviously been rebuilt and furnished. It also looked much larger in the torchlight.

Julian pulled her along, passing a suit of medieval armor and a tapestry of a war scene with fiery horses, glinting spears and swords and ferocious warriors. Glancing up, Caitlin suddenly had the distinct feeling that the eyes of the animals and the humans in the tapestry were following them.

If only.

She wished there was someone around to come to her rescue!

Thinking she herself would fight to the death with tooth and nail before Julian laid either hand or blade upon her, she stumbled, almost falling, when he halted to stare down into a great, deep, dark pit in the floor. Mounds of dirt rose on either side.

A grave?

Chills ran up and down her spine.

"Ah, no human has seen the cairn for more than a thousand years." He raised the dirk. "I, Atholl, have come to claim my heritage! The golden armor shall be mine! I shall go and come forth from the invisible world as I choose!"

Thunder rumbled in the distance, muted by the broch's thick walls. A torch hissed, and Caitlin blinked as a suit of armor came alive. No, not a full suit of armor... merely greaves that covered Bain's shins, and a shiny gold breastplate over his chest. His claymore was raised, and his expression was fierce.

A warrior in gold and black!

"Bain!"

"Fiend!" Julian jerked back, visibly shaken. "Get away from me! I killed you!"

"Not quite." Bain looked from his enemy to Caitlin. "Release the lady."

Sweat beading his face, Julian backed away, taking her with him. Then, obviously recognizing the opportunity she presented, he grabbed her, placing the blade of the dirk against her throat. "Surely you jest, prince. You can't order me to do anything! Step back, lay down your sword instantly, or I'll slit her throat right in front of you!"

She could feel the sharp edge of the dagger. Something warm slid down her throat—blood? But her eyes were on Bain, who backed away, his expression torn. She couldn't let him drop his weapon! She'd gotten herself into this situation, and she wouldn't let him suffer for it!

Desperate, she screeched, "The falcon!"

Julian jumped and looked upward, his hold on her weakening.

Taking the only chance she had, she bit his dirk hand as hard as she could and elbowed him with all her might.

"Yah!" he yelled, dropping the dagger.

Squirming away, she plunged forward, heading for the other side of the room.

But Julian was faster, and he was right on her tail. Lunging, the dagger once again in his hand, he swiped at her, knocking her into the wall. She grabbed the edge of a tapestry, staring up with horror as it tumbled. The heavy pole came down, hitting her squarely in the head.

She opened her eyes again in complete blackness. Was she dead? But then she moved slightly, smelled the earth beneath her, felt the heaviness of the fabric covering her. Knocked out by its pole, she lay beneath the fallen tapestry.

But how much time had passed?

Outside, she heard muffled curses and the clash of metal. Julian and Bain were fighting!

She scrambled out into the light and shakily got to her feet. She couldn't see the dueling men, couldn't even hear them, for thunder rumbled so loud the floor seemed to shake. She felt dizzy, sick, but she had to help Bain. Hurrying across the room, she finally sighted the men on the other side of the deep pit. Sword in one hand, dirk in the other, Julian thrust, parried, jumped back and thrust again. Despite his injuries, he seemed very skilled.

But Bain had him on the run. "Give up, Atholl! You are outmatched!"

"I'd rather die!"

"You *will* die."

"Aha!" Julian snarled, running at Bain with his sword.

Bain feinted, then followed when Julian turned and ran. Fearing the man would grab her again, Caitlin ducked below the mound of dirt.

"To the invisible world!" yelled Julian, laughing crazily.

Caitlin heard a muffled thud. She rose in time to watch Bain leap into the pit, presumably following Julian. The maniac's crazy laughter boomed from somewhere below.

The pit was obviously a tunnel. Peering over the edge, not knowing where the tunnel might lead, Caitlin decided she'd have to follow, too. What if Julian cornered the man she loved? The man who loved her? She jumped, tumbling as she hit the ground at least six feet below. Her head spun as she scrambled to her feet, but she kept going, ducking her head as she entered the narrow tunnel, and scurrying down a slanted incline.

Down and down. Deep, black darkness.

Earth sifted about her, giving her the creeps. But dim light burned farther on, and something white glowed in the tunnel's wall. She paused to glance at the white thing as she passed by. She felt her skin crawling when she recognized a human skull! She forced herself to look at it more closely, to see that it wore a helmet and was attached to a body curled up in some sort of a niche. Bony fingers rested on a sword.

My God! She had entered the legendary Celtic cairn on which Black Broch sat! An ancient mass grave.

But skeletons could do no harm to her or to Bain.

And Julian could!

His crazy laughter still echoed from below. She only wished he'd freak out completely, spasm into a catatonic state. Unfortunately, he was probably the type of psychotic who became as strong as three or four men twice his size. The laughter grew louder as she suddenly came out of the tunnel. And swords clashed. Bain and Julian fought desperately in a great, round area built like a beehive in stone.

Torches burning on the walls revealed more skeletons in niches all around. The nearest was that of a lady who still wore her elaborate golden spiral jewelry. Next to her lay another warrior, hands on his gold-hilted sword.

Gold! The cairn was full of it! Caitlin's eyes picked up the torchlit sheen of innumerable golden objects lying in niches and on the floor.

But her only concern was for Bain!

She gazed at the skeleton with the sword, planning to pluck the weapon from its fingers.

"You will not stop me!" Julian suddenly shouted. Then he lapsed into some sort of rhythmic Gaelic.

Bain roared and raised his sword, only to have it knocked from his hands.

"No!" Caitlin ran for the fallen weapon and threw it to Bain.

The next moment, Julian snarled and sent his claymore whizzing through the air to slam into the earth mere inches from her. She jumped back, her heart pounding. But then she seized the heavy sword and pulled it out, ready to do battle.

"Slit my throat, will you?" she yelled.

But now Julian was paying no attention to either her or Bain. His face rapt, he ran toward the wall, shouting in Gaelic.

"You will be sorry!" Bain shouted.

Thunder rumbled. Or was it an earthquake? Silently Caitlin prayed that the walls wouldn't cave in. They were so far underground!

"The door! The door!" chanted Julian, dancing around.

"Stupid fool!" said Bain.

Why wasn't he doing anything, now that he had the drop on the other man? Instead, he lowered his sword and turned to look at her, while behind him a great door seemed to be opening. Caitlin stared, openmouthed, as golden light spilled out. Then grass and trees appeared, greener and more delicate than she'd ever seen in her life.

"Go!" Bain yelled to her, pointing back the way they'd come.

But she stood rooted to the spot, her nerveless fingers letting the sword drop.

And Julian ran into the golden light, faltering only as his body began to waver in grotesque patterns, to shimmer in painful rhythms... until he started screaming in agony... and disintegrated into dust.

Bain took hold of the great door and, with a groan, pushed. "Run, Caitlin! He's dead! And all hell is going to break loose!"

But she was pinned to the spot. She saw riders in the distance, horses drifting through the incredibly green foliage. Sweet bells rang, hounds bayed. And she was very, very dizzy.

The door suddenly slammed shut!

And Bain was beside her. "I told you to go! I canna stop them—they will be out for any mortal's blood!"

She awoke as from a dream. "If I'm going, it'll be with you!"

You would have to take your pure sweet love and travel through the grave, into death itself.

On instinct, she reached for the bejeweled claymore, tearing it from his hand.

"Caitlin!"

"Come and get me!" she cried, running for the tunnel with the weapon, praying he'd follow.

She heard his heavy breathing as he gave chase. She ran like a stag before the hunters. She ran for her life.

And his.

A skeleton fell beneath her feet. Bones crunched. Dead fingers clutched at her ankles as the earth trembled viciously. The walls of the tunnel were caving in!

Seeing the opening in the floor above, Caitlin scrambled, clawed her way out of the pit, even as the dirt began to fall faster. She turned. "Bain!"

He was there, his hand outstretched. Grasping it, she pulled for all she was worth, but his feet slipped and his weight dragged her down.

"Let go!" he yelled. "Save yourself!"

"I love you!" she cried. "I'm not going to let you go!"

Trying again, struggling against the shifting earth, he scrambled out after her. At the same time, the pit closed in on itself with a great, dull roar. Clouds of dust rose to the very ceiling.

Coughing, choking, they sank into each other's arms. The room whirled and spun, and Caitlin could no longer keep her eyes open.

She came to, hearing the matter-of-fact voice of Sergeant Cooke.

"So a bump on the head and a few cuts are the worst of it, eh?" he said. "You are very, very lucky, Morghue. Trying to fight a vicious psychopath. Look at the way he killed poor Herbert Abernathy."

"Wanted for questioning in several ritualistic murders in London," put in one of the constables standing at Cooke's side. "Criminally insane. We brought it up on a computer in Inverary."

Bain smiled, adjusting the ice pack on Caitlin's head and stroking her hair when he noticed her eyes were open. "We are lucky indeed, especially that you came by and scared him off. I only wish that he hadna disappeared so fast."

Cooke sighed. "The storm helped hide him, I'm sure."

Caitlin remembered the storm, but she hadn't noticed any constables rushing in to scare off Julian. She also thought she remembered a sword battle, but, except for a small cut on his chin, Bain didn't seem any the worse for it.

Befuddled and disoriented, she swiveled her gaze about the great reception hall. How had they gotten upstairs? How had she come to be lying on the mahogany leather couch, resting in Bain's arms?

Multiple tapers burned in a candelabra on the table. But the light was still dim, and Sergeant Cooke was squinting as he filled out his report.

He focused on Caitlin. "We're here because the MacDonalds called to say you were missing, young lady. You can thank them for that. When we investigated, we found Julian Taylor's cottage trashed, his mirror shattered, and him missing. Mary MacDonald feared he might have killed you, too."

She struggled to find her voice. "H-how did you get in here?"

The sergeant raised his sandy brows. "Why, the same way the madman entered—the door was open." He gave Bain a hard look. "Are you sure she's all right, Morghue? She might have a concussion."

"The tapestry pole that struck her was light, but I will take her to a doctor, if you think it best."

Cooke waved his pen, as if suggesting Bain use his own judgment. "Watch her pupils. And don't let her fall asleep for several hours." He asked Caitlin, "Do you have a headache, lass?"

"No." Though her mind certainly felt gooey. She could hardly focus.

The sergeant stood. "I should be going. We have things to do, a lot more country to search. Some men from Scotland Yard are in Droon itself, you know. We have to check with the airports and all the boat and ship companies, though they're already looking for Taylor."

"Here's his picture," said a helpful constable, flashing a photo of Julian before her. Sleek hair, ordinary eyes, a smooth, good-looking face smiling pleasantly.

Caitlin recalled that hair standing on end, those eyes blazing, that mouth snarling, that face horribly disfigured by terrible scars. And she suddenly also remembered Julian screaming as...he... Had he really disappeared into thin air?

"My God!" she said with a shudder, knocking the ice pack off. "I remember—"

Bain tightened his hold on her and kissed her forehead. "Do not worry, my heart, everything is all right now." His voice was firm. "And we shall bolt the doors as soon as the constables have left."

Sergeant Cooke smiled. "So you two are engaged, are you?"

Engaged? Caitlin widened her eyes, feeling as if she'd awakened in some other time and place—and, possibly, some other planet.

Or had the other visions been the dream?

Cooke leaned over her. "You still look a bit confused, lass. But Laird Morghue here assures me he'll be taking good care of you. We'll go, if you'll nae be needing us."

She nodded. "He'll take care of me." Of *that* she was sure.

"We'll be stopping by the MacDonalds' to tell them you are all right," said the sergeant.

Letting Caitlin lie back against the cushions and replacing the ice pack, Bain walked the policemen to the door and out into the passageway. Voices drifted back to her.

"So you're newly returned to the area?" remarked Sergeant Cooke. "Well, what a fine renovation you are doing, Morghue. This old castle will be quite a tourist attraction when you are through."

"I am not sure 'twill be open to the public. I am thinking to keep it our own home."

"Still, it'll be some sight from outside, even from the road."

"But you'll be needing a telephone," added a constable. "Would have made it easier to reach you."

"We shall be getting one very soon," said Bain reassuringly, before all the voices faded as they continued toward the outer door.

Telephones? Tourist attractions? What was he talking about? To heck with the ice pack. Caitlin pulled herself up into a sitting position and heard something crackling in her sweater pocket. She delved into it and pulled out the little sketch of the male-female medallion. She'd forgotten she had it. She did a double take when she saw that the faces were finished.

How had that happened? And the man looked like Bain, the woman like her!

Footsteps sounded in the hall, and Bain came in, frowning. "Lie back down, lass. You should be resting."

But she was too excited. "Look at this!"

He stopped by the couch and took the sketch from her. "Aye, very nicely done. A good-luck token meant to keep you safe."

"But I swear the faces weren't finished when I first picked it up. I had it in my pocket all this time."

Bain didn't react to the puzzle of the faces. Instead, he suggested, "Perhaps the medallion helped protect you from Julian Taylor."

Julian. Again she flashed on him disappearing in golden light. "H-he disintegrated."

"He is gone. 'Tis all that matters." The blue of his eyes glimmered in the firelight as he leaned over her. The frown darkened to a scowl. "A lump the size of an egg. Bastard! He deserved to disintegrate for laying even one finger on you!"

She felt her head, remembering the falling tapestry, wondering what else had actually happened and what she'd hallucinated. The changed faces on the medallion were the least of many strange things....

But her memory had many holes. She couldn't recall anything about agreeing to be engaged.

"Did you propose to me?"

He looked startled. "You dinna remember it?"

She shook her head, then winced. "Just a lot of yelling and fighting when we were down in the cairn." She stiffened. "The cairn under Black Broch—it exists!"

"Not anymore. 'Tis caved in," said Bain hurriedly. "And I have to admit, I am relieved that any museum or thief would have to dig for miles to find anything. My family has a superstition about the gold and such staying here, but at least I no longer have to guard it every minute."

He was only guarding gold? Again she struggled to understand, as memories flitted through her mind. "What about...the door?"

"Shh! You should really rest." He stroked her cheek. "And I am more concerned that you do not remember my romantic proposal."

"But I saw—"

"Stars, when that tapestry fell on you."

"But you're the—"

"Man who loves you," he cut in. "The man who owes you everything, brave, sweet Caitlin." He knelt, his expression taking her breath away. "So I shall ask you again—will you marry me? I have been waiting for you all my life."

"I've been waiting for you, too." True love. Mystery. Passion and courage. "Yes, of course I'll marry you."

She wasn't sure what would happen in the future, but she knew they belonged together, felt as if she'd gone through a great trial to win him.

They kissed, lips and hands touching, seeking, like the intertwining man and woman on the Celtic medallion. Male and female, the perfect balance. A beautiful, even-armed cross.

A never-ending knot that symbolized eternity.

EPILOGUE

The night Caitlin and Bain attended their engagement party at the MacDonalds' house began with clear moonlight, but soon turned to heavy mist and restless wind. Caitlin didn't care. She'd learned to appreciate the area's quicksilver atmosphere.

She'd also learned to appreciate the multiple facets of her husband-to-be over the past few weeks. Possessing several degrees, including one in ancient history, he was intelligently informed on many subjects, yet able to make small talk with the lowliest shepherd. Though very wealthy, he preferred a life of activity over one of leisure. Protective in an old-fashioned way, he still encouraged Caitlin to be a jewelry designer, had suggested new European markets, since she was going to stay in Scotland. His personality leaning toward brooding moods, he could nevertheless laugh and play, especially now that he had someone with whom to share his life.

But, despite their having lived together for so many days, Caitlin was quite aware of Bain Morghue's deep, abiding aura of mystery. She still wasn't certain about all she'd seen and experienced since meeting him, and it seemed she might never be sure.

She was thinking on that as they walked down the road from the manor house to Black Broch. The moon was a ghostly eye glowing through the fog, and a chill mist swirled about them. But Bain kept her warm and close, an arm slung around her shoulders.

"Did you see Tam and the other people from the Braemarton Fair at the party?" she asked.

"Aye."

"And the man with the blue snake tattoo?" His long hair and mustache braided, he'd been wearing a T-shirt with a picture of the Lochfynton standing stones and the words *Celtic Myth* silk-screened on it. "I don't believe he could speak any English, and he was positively devouring the refreshment table."

Bain laughed.

Caitlin poked him. "That man scared me. I saw him in the fairy rade with a human skull on his spear."

She waited for him to once again tell her she'd only been dreaming. But he remained silent, the wind feathering his hair around his handsome face.

"Now, I can understand Ghillie being at the party, and Tam, and some of the others," she went on. "But the snake-tattoo guy? I thought the door to the invisible world was closed." When she spoke as if unusual events were fact, she'd noticed, Bain gave her straighter answers. "*Is* the door closed?"

"There could be more than one door, sweet Caitlin."

"Oh, great."

"You need have no fear. You are in no danger." He added, "And my responsibility is over."

Though he'd seemed reluctant to commit to visiting her family in the States. Instead, he'd generously offered to pay their fares to the British Isles, suggesting they come as often as they liked.

He cleared his throat. "My mother may be coming to the wedding, you know."

Caitlin widened her eyes. "Is her name Morrighan? You've never said."

"Some call her Maggie. From all that she's heard, she has great respect for you."

"I hope so." And that her mother-in-law would get along with her parents. "What about your other relatives?"

"Some may come bringing gifts. Others we may not see until we produce a firstborn."

Caitlin experienced an odd thrill at the mention of a child. "Well, no one had best try to steal the babe away and make her spin gold, or some such."

Bain laughed long and loud. "What a wit you are, my heart. No one would have the nerve to come up against the bairn's mother."

She took a deep breath of relief and tightened her arm about his waist. "I'm not always sure...when I'm dealing with the extraordinary."

"Life is full of illusion."

"Especially *your* life."

"Which you now share." Bain sobered, gazing down at her. "You have a responsibility, you know, as one of the wise who can see beyond ordinary reality."

"Responsibility to use it as inspiration for my art?" That was something she looked forward to. "Or responsibility to keep it a secret?"

"Who would believe you?"

True, she could hardly believe it herself. "I only wish I could be certain about exactly what I'm seeing when I see it."

"There is no certainty. Which is as it should be. The fey wouldna be half so beautiful if they could not flit about the real world like phantoms."

Though his love was quite real. She trusted in that fully. Thinking about how happy she was to wake up in his arms every morning, she didn't pay attention to where she stepped.

"Are you all right, sweet Caitlin?"

"It's these high heels. I forgot to change to my walking shoes before we left. We need a car." She'd turned in her rental vehicle.

"Nae. A car is too ordinary." He whistled into the wind.

Seconds later, his nostrils steaming, the black stallion came galloping out of the fog, giving her a start. And when she really thought about it, Caitlin had to admit that she wanted to continue to be surprised by life. She'd come to Scotland for romance and myth and mystery beyond the ordinary world.

She'd found all that she'd longed for in her Prince of Air and Darkness. And she had no intention of losing her sense of wonder—or him—ever.

* * * * *

SPRING
fancy
'94

**They're sexy, single…
and about to get snagged!**

Passion is in full bloom as love catches
the fancy of three brash bachelors. You won't
want to miss these stories by three of
Silhouette's hottest authors:

**CAIT LONDON
DIXIE BROWNING
PEPPER ADAMS**

Spring fever is in the air this March—
and there's no avoiding it!

Only from

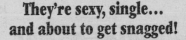

where passion lives.

Relive the romance...
Harlequin and Silhouette
are proud to present

by Request™

A program of collections of three complete novels by the most requested authors with the most requested themes. Be sure to look for one volume each month with three complete novels by top name authors.

In January: **WESTERN LOVING**   Susan Fox
JoAnn Ross
Barbara Kaye

Loving a cowboy is easy—taming him isn't!

In February: **LOVER, COME BACK!**   Diana Palmer
Lisa Jackson
Patricia Gardner Evans

It was over so long ago—yet now they're calling, "Lover, Come Back!"

In March: **TEMPERATURE RISING**   JoAnn Ross
Tess Gerritsen
Jacqueline Diamond

Falling in love—just what the doctor ordered!

Available at your favorite retail outlet.

REQ-G3

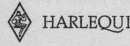

HARLEQUIN®   Silhouette

And now for
something completely different
from Silhouette....

SPELLBOUND
R O M A N C E

Unique and innovative stories that take you into the world of paranormal happenings. Look for our special "Spellbound" flash—and get ready for a truly exciting reading experience!

In February, look for
One Unbelievable Man (SR #993)
by Pat Montana.

Was he man or myth? Cass Kohlmann's mysterious traveling companion, Michael O'Shea, had her all confused. He'd suddenly appeared, claiming she was his destiny—determined to win her heart. But could levelheaded Cass learn to believe in fairy tales...before her fantasy man disappeared forever?

Don't miss the charming, sexy and utterly mysterious
Michael O'Shea in
ONE UNBELIEVABLE MAN.
Watch for him in February—only from

Silhouette
R O M A N C E™

SILHOUETTE... Where Passion Lives

Don't miss these Silhouette favorites by some of our most distinguished authors! And now you can receive a discount by ordering two or more titles!

SD	#05772	FOUND FATHER by Justine Davis	$2.89	❏
SD	#05783	DEVIL OR ANGEL by Audra Adams	$2.89	❏
SD	#05786	QUICKSAND by Jennifer Greene	$2.89	❏
SD	#05796	CAMERON by Beverly Barton	$2.99	❏
IM	#07481	FIREBRAND by Paula Detmer Riggs	$3.39	❏
IM	#07502	CLOUD MAN by Barbara Faith	$3.50	❏
IM	#07505	HELL ON WHEELS by Naomi Horton	$3.50	❏
IM	#07512	SWEET ANNIE'S PASS by Marilyn Pappano	$3.50	❏
SE	#09791	THE CAT THAT LIVED ON PARK AVENUE by Tracy Sinclair	$3.39	❏
SE	#09793	FULL OF GRACE by Ginna Ferris	$3.39	❏
SE	#09822	WHEN SOMEBODY WANTS by Trisha Alexander	$3.50	❏
SE	#09841	ON HER OWN by Pat Warren	$3.50	❏
SR	#08866	PALACE CITY PRINCE by Arlene James	$2.69	❏
SR	#08916	UNCLE DADDY by Kasey Michaels	$2.69	❏
SR	#08948	MORE THAN YOU KNOW by Phyllis Halldorson	$2.75	❏
SR	#08954	HERO IN DISGUISE by Stella Bagwell	$2.75	❏
SS	#27006	NIGHT MIST by Helen R. Myers	$3.50	❏
SS	#27010	IMMINENT THUNDER by Rachel Lee	$3.50	❏
SS	#27015	FOOTSTEPS IN THE NIGHT by Lee Karr	$3.50	❏
SS	#27020	DREAM A DEADLY DREAM by Allie Harrison	$3.50	❏

(limited quantities available on certain titles)

AMOUNT	$	
DEDUCT: **10% DISCOUNT FOR 2+ BOOKS**	$	
POSTAGE & HANDLING	$	_____
($1.00 for one book, 50¢ for each additional)		
APPLICABLE TAXES*	$	_____
TOTAL PAYABLE	$	_____
(check or money order—please do not send cash)		

To order, complete this form and send it, along with a check or money order for the total above, payable to Silhouette Books, to: **In the U.S.:** 3010 Walden Avenue, P.O. Box 9077, Buffalo, NY 14269-9077; **In Canada:** P.O. Box 636, Fort Erie, Ontario, L2A 5X3.

Name: _____

Address: _____ City: _____

State/Prov.: _____ Zip/Postal Code: _____

*New York residents remit applicable sales taxes.
Canadian residents remit applicable GST and provincial taxes.   SBACK-JM

Silhouette®

It's our 1000th
Silhouette Romance
and we're celebrating!

Join us for a special collection of love stories by the authors you've loved for years, and new favorites you've just discovered.

It's a celebration just for you,
with wonderful books by
Diana Palmer, Suzanne Carey,
Tracy Sinclair, Marie Ferrarella,
Debbie Macomber, Laurie Paige,
Annette Broadrick, Elizabeth August
and MORE!

Silhouette Romance...vibrant, fun and emotionally rich! Take another look at us!

As part of the celebration, readers can receive a FREE gift AND enter our exciting sweepstakes to win a grand prize of $1000! Look for more details in all March Silhouette series titles.

You'll fall in love all over again
with Silhouette Romance!